MEMO

To: Matthias Barton
From: Kendall Scarborough
Re: My Resignation

Following up on our earlier conversation, I am hereby submitting my resignation. While I have enjoyed my five years as your personal assistant, I feel it is time for me to move on to an opportunity where my qualifications can be used to their fullest. I am sure you will find someone who can program your BlackBerry, make your coffee and organize your office to your liking.

Please rest assured that my resignation is solely for professional purposes and has nothing to do with your engagement, your unengagement or any other personal matters. The timing is strictly coincidental.

Dear Reader,

Whenever you get a group of writers together, something interesting always develops. Something like, oh...I don't know, a romance series. That's what happened with the book you're reading now. When some of us gathered in a hotel room at a romance writers' conference and called another writer on the phone, we somehow ended up brainstorming what would become Desire's MILLIONAIRE OF THE MONTH series.

We came home from the conference and immediately formed an e-mail loop, and little by little, the series took shape. One of us even located a magazine featuring log homes that included the perfect lodge for the Seven Samurai to occupy in the stories.

I had so much fun working with the other writers on this series, and I loved how it all turned out. Here's hoping you enjoy our millionaires, as well.

Happy reading!

Elizabeth Bevarly

ELIZABETH BEVARLY

MARRIED TO HIS BUSINESS

Published by Silhouette Books
America's Publisher of Contemporary Romance

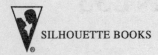

SILHOUETTE BOOKS

ISBN-13: 978-0-373-76809-7
ISBN-10:   0-373-76809-5

MARRIED TO HIS BUSINESS

Recent Books by Elizabeth Bevarly

Silhouette Desire

First Comes Love #1323
Monahan's Gamble #1337
The Temptation of Rory Monahan #1363
When Jayne Met Erik #1389
The Secret Life of Connor Monahan #1406
Taming the Prince #1474
Taming the Beastly MD #1501
Married to His Business #1809

Harlequin Blaze

Indecent Suggestion #189
My Only Vice #273

HQN Books

Express Male
You've Got Male

ELIZABETH BEVARLY

is a *New York Times* bestselling, award-winning author of more than fifty novels and eight novellas. Her books have been published in nineteen languages and more than two dozen countries, and have been included in Harlequin launches in Russia, China and the Spanish-speaking North American market. There are more than eight million copies of her books in print worldwide.

Although she has claimed as residences Washington, DC; Virginia; New Jersey and Puerto Rico, she now resides back in her native Kentucky with her husband and son, where she fully intends to remain.

For all my Desire readers over the years.
Thanks for joining me on the ride.

One

As Kendall Scarborough watched her boss close his cell phone, stride to the northernmost window of his office and push it open, then hurl the apparatus into the wild blue yonder, she found herself thinking that maybe, just maybe, this wasn't a good day to tender her resignation. Again. But she would. Again. And this time she would make it stick.

And how fitting that one of her last tasks for Matthias Barton would be ordering him a new phone. Again. At least phones were easier to program and format to his liking than were PDAs and MP3 players, a number of which also lay at the bottom of the reflecting pool in the courtyard of Barton Limited—which just so happened to be situated directly below the northernmost window of Matthias's office. In fact, there were at least five years' worth of PDAs and MP3 players and other small appa-ratuses…apparati…little gizmos…in the pool, Kendall knew. Matthias Barton was, without question, one of the finest minds working in big business today. But when it came to itty-bitty pieces of machinery, he was reduced to, well…throwing a lot of stuff out the window.

She straightened her little black-framed glasses and plucked out the pen that was perpetually tucked into the tidy, dark blond bun knotted at the back of her head. Then she withdrew a small notepad from the pocket of the charcoal pin-striped, man-style trousers she'd paired with a tailored white, man-style shirt. All of her work clothes were man-style, because she was convinced they gave her petite, five-foot-four-inch frame a more imposing presence in the male-dominated society of big business. After scribbling a few notes—not the least of which was *New phone for Matthias*—she flipped the notepad closed and stuffed it back into her pocket.

"Kendall," he began as he closed the window and latched it, then turned to make his way back to his desk.

"Got it covered, sir," she told him before he said another word. "We'll go with VeraWave this time. I'm sure that service will suit you much better than the last one."

To herself, she added, *And the one before that. And the one before that. And the one before that.* It was just a good thing Barton Limited was headquartered in a city like San Francisco where new phone services sprang up every day. The year wasn't even half over, and Kendall had already been forced to change cellular companies three times.

"Thank you," Matthias told her as he seated himself behind his big mahogany desk and reached for the small stack of letters she'd typed up that morning, which were now awaiting his signature.

His attire was, of course, man-style, too, but she didn't

think that was what gave him such an imposing presence—
though certainly the espresso-colored suit and dark gold
dress shirt and tie, coupled with his dark hair and even
darker eyes, didn't diminish it. Matthias himself was just
larger than life, be it sitting at the head of the massive table
that bisected the boardroom of Barton Limited, or slamming a squash ball into the wall at his athletic club, or
charming some bastion of society into a major investment
at a dinner party. Kendall had seen him in each of those
situations—and dozens of others—and she couldn't think
of a single moment when Matthias *hadn't* been imposing.

He'd intimidated the hell out of her when she'd first
come to work for him straight out of graduate school, even
though, back then, he'd barely been out of grad school
himself. In spite of his youth, he'd already made millions,
several times over. Kendall had been awed that someone
only five years older than she—Matthias had only recently
turned thirty-two—was already light-years ahead of her on
the corporate ladder. She'd wanted to observe his habits
and policies and procedures and mimic them, thinking she
could achieve the same rapid rise and level of success
through emulation.

It hadn't taken long, however, for her to realize she would
never be in Matthias's league. He was too focused, too
intense, too driven. His work was his life. He needed it to
survive as much as he did oxygen or food. Over time, she'd
gotten used to his ruthless single-mindedness when it came
to achieving success, even if she'd never been able to understand it. And not just any old run-of-the-mill success, either.
No, Matthias Barton had to be the absolute, no-close-
seconds, unparalleled *best* at everything he set out to do.

Not that it mattered now, Kendall told herself, since she

wasn't going to be a part of his pursuit—or his success—much longer. She had a pursuit—and success—of her own to accomplish, and she should have started years ago. With her MBA from Stanford, she'd been overqualified for the position of personal assistant when she'd taken the job with Matthias. But she'd known that working for someone like him for a couple of years, even as a personal assistant, would offer her *entrée* into an echelon of big business that most recent grads never saw. She'd learn from a legend and make contacts up the wazoo, swimming with the proverbial sharks. But "a couple of years" had become five, and Kendall was savvy enough around the sharks now to be able to grill them up with a nice wasabi sauce.

It was time to go.

"Okay, where were we?" Matthias asked.

"Well, sir," she began, "you'd just, um, concluded your call with Elliot Donovan at The Springhurst Corporation, and I—" She inhaled a deep breath, steeled herself for battle, and said, in a surprisingly sturdy voice, "I was about to give you my two weeks' notice." To herself, she added silently, *And this time, I'm going through with it, no matter how hard you try to change my mind.*

His head snapped up at her announcement, and his bittersweet chocolate eyes went flinty. "Kendall, I thought we'd already talked about this."

"We have, sir, several times," she agreed. "Which is why it shouldn't come as a surprise. Now that your wedding to Miss Conover is off—"

"Look, just because Lauren and I canceled our plans," Matthias interrupted, "that doesn't mean I don't still need you to take care of things."

His now-defunct wedding to Lauren Conover had just

been the most recent reason he'd used for why Kendall couldn't leave his employ yet, but she was still surprised he would try to use it again. Technically, the wedding hadn't been canceled. There had just been a change of date and venue. Oh, and also a change of groom, since Lauren was now planning to marry Matthias's twin brother, Luke.

"Anything left to do will be taken care of by Miss Conover and her family," Kendall pointed out. "If there's anything left to do."

And she doubted there was. Matthias hadn't spoken much about his broken engagement, but Kendall hadn't been surprised when she'd heard the news. Well, maybe the part about Lauren's falling in love with Luke Barton had been a little surprising. Okay, a lot surprising. But even without Luke's intervention, the marriage, as far as Kendall was concerned, would have been a huge mistake. Matthias had proposed to Lauren Conover only because he'd wanted to merge his business with her father's, and Lauren Conover had accepted the proposal only because…

Well, frankly, Kendall was still trying to figure that one out. She'd met Lauren only a few times, but she'd never gotten the impression that Lauren was in love with Matthias—or even in like with him. Obviously she hadn't been in love, because she wouldn't have fallen for his brother, identical twin or not, if she had been. Personality-wise, Luke and Matthias Barton couldn't be more different from each other—save the fact that Luke was as driven professionally as his brother was. At least, that was what the office scuttlebutt said. Kendall had never met the other man in person.

There was no question that the match between Luke and Lauren was indeed a love match. With Matthias, however, any life he'd envisioned building with Lauren had been more about business than pleasure, more about ambition than affection. There were times when Kendall wondered if the man could care about anything *but* building his business.

Matthias said nothing for a moment, only met Kendall's gaze levelly. "But there are other things I'm going to need you to—"

"There is nothing," she quickly, but firmly, interjected, before he had a chance to create and/or fabricate a host of obligations that anyone could see to. "We're coming up on the slowest time of the year for Barton Limited," she reminded him. "I have you up to speed on everything for the next month. Now that the Stuttgart trip is out of the way, you don't have any international travel scheduled until the fall. No conferences until September. Nothing pressing that whoever you hire to take my place won't have plenty of time to prepare for. And since you'll be spending the entire month of July at your friend's lodge, anyway, that makes this the perfect time for me to—"

"I'll need you more than ever at Hunter's lodge," Matthias interrupted. "Even with all the preparation I've done—"

You mean *I've* done, Kendall thought to herself, since it had been she, not Matthias, who'd made all the arrangements.

"—it's still going to be difficult, being away from the office for that length of time. It's essential that I take someone with me who knows what's going on."

"Then I'd suggest you take Douglas Morton," Kendall said, naming one of Barton Limited's newest VPs.

"Morton needs to be here," Matthias said. "*You* need to be with me."

So now he was going to use the mysterious month at the

mysterious lodge to keep her on her leash, Kendall thought. She knew his upcoming trip to his friend's lodge on Lake Tahoe was much more than a trip to his friend's lodge on Lake Tahoe, even if she had no idea exactly why. All she knew was that, in January, he'd received a letter out of the blue from some law office representing the estate of a friend of his from college. The man had passed away, but before going had imparted a dying wish he wanted fulfilled by his old friends. They were each to spend one month in a lodge he owned on the lake.

Why? Kendall had no idea. But Matthias had driven her crazy for weeks, trying to rearrange his spring schedule so that he could spend his assigned month of April in Lake Tahoe. Then, when he'd been unable to reschedule a trip to Germany in April, he'd driven her even crazier rearranging everything she'd spent weeks rearranging so that he could switch months with his brother Luke—whom he hadn't even spoken to in years at that point—who had been assigned July.

There were seven friends in all, Kendall knew, dating back to Matthias's time at Harvard, all of whom had gradually lost touch with one another after graduating. Matthias hadn't wanted to talk about it in detail, and Kendall had respected his wishes. She'd also managed the impossible, reworking his schedule and obligations—twice—so that he could abide by his friend's last wishes and spend his month in Lake Tahoe.

It would have been so much better if he'd been able to stick with the original plan. Not only because she would have saved herself a lot of trouble, but because Lake Tahoe was where Kendall would be going to complete the necessary training for her new job—starting the first week of

July. She was dreading the possibility—however remote—that she might run into Matthias there so soon after severing ties with him. He was bound to be unhappy about her leaving. Even more so once he discovered who her new employer was.

"I can't be with you, sir," she reiterated. Inhaling a deep breath, she told him the rest. "I've been offered a position elsewhere that I've already accepted. They want me to take part in a week-long training seminar that starts the first of July—two weeks from today," she added for emphasis. "And I'll report for work at the company immediately after completing my orientation."

Matthias said nothing for several moments, only leaned back in his chair and crossed his arms over his expansive chest. Then he looked at her in a way that made Kendall feel like her backbone was dissolving. Fast. Finally, he said, "You've already accepted a position somewhere else?"

She nodded. And she hoped she sounded more confident than she suddenly felt when she told him, "Um, yes?"

Oh, yeah. That sounded totally confident. There was nothing like punctuating a statement with a question mark to really hammer home one's point. Provided one was a four-year-old child.

"Mind telling me where?" he asked.

Kendall braced herself for his reaction, reminding herself to be forceful and assertive and end her sentences with a period. Maybe even an exclamation point where necessary. By golly. Or, rather, By Golly! "With, um, OmniTech Solutions?" she said. Asked. Whatever. Oh, hell. "I'm going to be their new VP? In charge of Public Relations?" When she realized she was still speaking in the inquisitive tense, Kendall closed her eyes and mentally willed her age back up to twenty-seven-and-a-half. If she kept this up, Matthias wouldn't let her have her milk and cookies for snack later.

When she opened her eyes again, she saw that his dark brows had shot up even farther at her declaration. Question. Whatever. Oh, hell.

"OmniTech?" he asked. Using the proper punctuation, Kendall couldn't help noticing. Unlike *some* people. "Who the hell recruited you to work for OmniTech?"

Strange that he would assume she was recruited, she thought, and that she hadn't gone looking for the position on her own. Even if, you know, she had been recruited for the position and hadn't gone looking for it on her own. "Stephen DeGallo," she told him. And she applauded herself for finally grasping the proper rules of punctuation. Now if she could just do something about the sudden drop in volume her voice had taken….

Although she wouldn't have thought it possible, Matthias's eyebrows arched even higher. "The CEO of the company recruited you to come work for him?" he asked with obvious disbelief. "As a vice president?"

Kendall didn't see what was so unbelievable about that. She was perfectly qualified for the job. Tamping down her irritation, she repeated, "Yes, sir."

Matthias narrowed his eyes at her. "Stephen DeGallo never hires from outside the company. He always promotes from within. He doesn't trust outsiders. He likes to surround himself with people he's trained to think like he does. You know. Suck-ups."

Kendall ignored the comment. Mostly because she couldn't help thinking that, after five years of working for Matthias, she was even better qualified for the job of suck-up than she was vice president in charge of public relations. "Stephen said—"

"Stephen?" Matthias echoed, this time punctuating the comment with an incredulous expulsion of air. "You're already calling him by his first name?"

"He insisted. Sir," Kendall added meaningfully, since Matthias had never extended her the invitation to address him so informally, even after being his right-hand woman for five years. Before he could comment further, she hurried on, "Stephen said I had impeccable credentials. And I do," she couldn't help adding. "In case you've forgotten, I have an MBA from Stanford, and I graduated with highest honors."

Matthias actually smiled at that. "Oh, yeah, I'll just bet DeGallo's impressed with your…credentials." He leaned back in his chair even more, folding his arms now to cradle his head in his hands. It was a position Kendall knew well, one that was meant to lull the observer into a false sense of security before Matthias struck with the velocity and toxicity of a cobra.

"You realize," he said, "that the only reason DeGallo offered you the job is because he's competing with Barton Limited for the Perkins contract, and he's going to expect you to tell him everything you know about the work we've done so far to win it."

The barb hit home, just as she knew Matthias had meant for it to. Instead of reacting to it, however, Kendall only replied calmly, "That would be highly unethical, sir. Possibly even criminal. Not only could Stephen *not* be expecting me to provide him with any such information, but he must know I'd never betray you that way."

"Wouldn't you?" Matthias asked easily.

Kendall gaped at him. Now that was a reaction she *hadn't* expected. "Of course I wouldn't. How can you even ask me something like that?"

She realized then how right she'd been to accept the new position. If Matthias could suspect she was capable of turning on him so completely, so readily, then he truly didn't view her any differently than he did the phones he tossed out the window. He'd also implied she wasn't qualified for her new job, even after the countless times she'd proved how valuable an employee she was.

Clearly, it was time to go.

"Fine, then," he said, dropping his arms and sitting up straight again. "But, Kendall, haven't you learned anything from me in the time you've been at Barton Limited? Big business isn't the gentleman's game it was a generation ago. No one's going to do you any favors. Why should you do any favors for them? For me? When it comes to business, you think of yourself first, others not at all. Feel free to report to OmniTech tomorrow if you want. Since you'll be going to work for one of my competitors, I can't risk having you around the office any longer and potentially compromising the work we're doing here. Your two weeks' notice won't be necessary. You're fired. Clear out your desk immediately. I'll have Sarah call security and they can escort you out of the building. You have ten minutes."

And with that, he turned his attention back to the stack of papers requiring his signature and began to sign each without another glance in her direction.

Kendall had no idea what to say. She hadn't expected this from Matthias at all. She'd thought he would react the way he'd reacted every other time she'd tried to resign, with a seemingly endless list of reasons why she couldn't go, none of which was in any way legitimate. Never in a million years would she have thought he would fire her, even if she was going to work for one of his competitors. Barton Limited had scores of competitors. She would have been hard-pressed to find a position with a company that *didn't* compete with Matthias in some way. She'd thought he would view her acceptance of a new job the same way she did: as business. Instead, he seemed to have taken it…

Personally, she marveled.

Immediately, she told herself that was impossible. Matthias Barton didn't get personal. About anything. He was just reacting this way because he was worried she would compromise his pursuit of the Perkins contract. That, she thought, *wasn't* surprising. That he would think of his business first, and others…well, as he'd said, not at all. She just wished he had enough faith in her to realize that she would never do anything to sabotage him or his work.

Clearly, it was *so* time to go.

With a briskly muttered "Yes, sir," Kendall spun on her heel and exited Matthias's office, giving him the same courtesy he'd extended to her and not looking back once. She wasn't the kind of person to look backward. Only forward. That was the reason she'd come to work for Matthias in the first place, because she'd been thinking ahead, to a better future. Now that future was the present. It was time to start thinking forward again. And that meant never giving another thought to…

Well. She could barely remember Matthias Thaddeus Barton's name. Or how his espresso eyes flashed gold when he was angry. Or how that one unruly lock of dark hair fell forward whenever he had his head bent in concentration. Or how one side of his mouth turned up more than another whenever he smiled that arrogant smile…

Matthias looked at the closed door through which Kendall had just exited and silently cursed it for ruining the view. Not that there was anything especially scenic about Kendall Scarborough. With her librarian glasses and those mannish, colorless clothes hiding what was doubtless a curve-free body, anyway, and with her hair always bound tightly to her head, she wasn't likely to be showing up as a trifold with staples taped inside the locker of a dockworker. Of course, that had been the first thing to grab his attention during her interview five years ago, because the last thing he'd wanted or needed in a personal assistant was someone he might want to get personal with.

Not that *personal* to Matthias was all that personal, but the risk for screwing up was always there, since he had, in the past, been swayed by beauty, with disastrous results. He was understandably wary around beautiful things and beautiful women. But he'd never been able to resist either.

He'd thought he'd solved his problem by arranging a marriage with Lauren Conover that would have provided him with not just a suitable wife for a man in his position, but a beneficial merger with her father's company, as well. Lauren was beautiful, smart, accomplished and chic, but there hadn't been a spark of any inconvenient passion between them. The two of them could have lived in a beautiful home, had beautiful children and a beautiful life, without Matthias ever having to get too deeply involved with any of it. It had been so perfect. Until his brother, Luke, had come along and, as had been a habit with Lunkhead since their childhood, screwed up a perfectly good thing.

But it wasn't Lunkhead Luke who had screwed up things with Kendall, Matthias reminded himself. Kendall, who was exactly what Matthias *did* want and need in a personal assistant: pragmatic and professional, enterprising and efficient. In the five years she'd worked for him, she'd been his calendar, his clock, his coordinator. His bartender, his astrologer, his conscience. His butcher, his baker, his candlestick maker. His tinker, his tailor, his spy.

That last word hit Matthias hard, since it was precisely what he'd just accused Kendall of being for someone else. Even though he knew she wouldn't. Even though he knew she couldn't. Although there was no question that Stephen DeGallo's motive in hiring her had been driven by his hope—hell, his certainty—that he could persuade her to share information about both Matthias and Barton Limited that would work to his benefit, Matthias couldn't honestly see her turning on him that way. He'd just been so surprised by her announcement that she'd already accepted a job somewhere else—and with his biggest competitor—that he hadn't known what to say.

Whenever she'd tried to tender her resignation before, Matthias had always been able to talk her out of it. And he'd always talked her out of it because he'd needed her here. Hell, he knew she was overqualified for her position. That was why he'd given her so many raises over the years that she was now making almost twice what her predecessors had made. Yeah, okay, maybe she could be doing more with her degree and her savvy, he conceded reluctantly. But she didn't have to do it for OmniTech.

There was no way Stephen DeGallo had recruited

Kendall for her résumé. He didn't see her the way Matthias did—pragmatic and professional, enterprising and efficient. She was just an opportunity to mine the practices and policies of Barton Limited. Nothing more.

He expelled a disgruntled breath of air as he continued to look at the closed door. Well, he'd just have to get along without her, wouldn't he? He'd just hire another personal assistant, that was all. Someone else who was pragmatic and professional, enterprising and efficient. Someone else who would be his calendar, clock and conscience. That shouldn't be so hard, right? He'd put Kendall on it right away.

His finger was actually on the buzzer to call her in before he realized what he'd been about to do. Ask Kendall, the woman he'd just fired—not to mention insulted—to hire a replacement for herself. He shook his head and chuckled at himself for the gaffe, even if he couldn't find anything especially funny about it. Man. If he didn't know better, he'd almost think he couldn't do *anything* without Kendall. And that, he knew, was nuts.

He was a captain of industry. He had made his first million less than a year after graduating from college, and he'd multiplied it dozens of times over since. He headed a Fortune 500 Company that employed thousands of people all over the world.

So he'd lost his personal assistant, he thought. So what? Personal assistants were as easy to find as cheap champagne on New Year's Eve. He'd hire another one tomorrow. Have the person trained well enough by the time he left for Tahoe that they would at least have the basics down. Actually, the timing, as Kendall had said, was perfect. He could use the month in Tahoe with his new assistant to mold him or her to his liking.

Matthias would get along just fine without Kendall Scarborough. Hell, yes, he would.

Hell, yes.

Two

Kendall made the trip to Tahoe courtesy of OmniTech, enjoying the brief flight in first class. A rental car awaited her on arrival, a luxury sedan that was quite the posh way to travel, compared to her little economy car at home. Maybe on her new salary, she could ultimately buy something like this, she thought as she settled into the leather seat and pushed the button to open the sunroof. As the balmy summer air tumbled into the car, she donned her sunglasses, fastened her seat belt over her white oxford shirt and khaki trousers and tuned the radio to the jazz station. Then, feeling like a corporate executive for the first time in her life, she pulled out of the rental lot at the airport basking in contentment.

Until she thought about Matthias Barton. Then her contentment fled. And what she'd hoped would be a peaceful, introspective drive that was filled with planning for her future at OmniTech suddenly turned into a grueling marathon of disgruntlement instead.

But then, thoughts of Matthias—never mind disgruntlement—had been regular companions over the two weeks that had passed since she'd last seen him. So as she merged onto the highway, Kendall did her best to think of something—anything—else. How she needed to replace the hardware on her kitchen cabinets. The fact that women's shoe manufacturers still hadn't figured out how to wed style with comfort. Why the sky was blue and the grass was green. The atomic weight of boron. Where the contestants of *Survivor* should go next—though, admittedly, it probably wasn't polite for her to say aloud where *she* thought they should go. Whatever it took to keep from hearing again those two little words she'd never thought she'd hear Matthias say to her.

You're fired.

She still couldn't believe he'd done it. After giving him five years of her life, years she could have spent building her own career instead of bolstering his, he'd cut her loose in the most insulting way possible. She'd seen him fire plenty of people during the time she'd worked for him, but they were people who'd deserved the boot. Employees who had been, at best, ineffective, and at worst, dishonest. People who had cheated him, or lied to him, or stolen from him. Now Kendall, who had never missed a day on the job, and whose work ethic had been irreproachable, had been relegated to their ranks.

But even that wasn't what bothered her the most. What bothered her the most was her own reaction to having been fired. She told herself she should be angry with Matthias for the way he'd dismissed her. She should be resentful.

She should be outraged. She should be reporting him to the Equal Opportunity Commission. Instead, what she felt was hurt. Hurt in the same way a little girl feels hurt when she's always picked last for kickball. And hurt feelings were *not* something a consummate professional like Kendall should feel.

Matthias was right about one thing. She hadn't learned as much from him as she'd thought she would when she accepted the position, if she couldn't be the focused, unflinching businesswoman she'd envisioned becoming. She could be as ruthless and determined as Matthias was, she told herself. She *could*. And she would be, too. Starting the moment she passed through the doors of the Timber Lake Inn.

That must be a new hotel in Tahoe, Kendall thought as she exited onto the road that would take her to her final destination. She'd never heard of it before. It was kind of an odd name for a conference hotel, too. They must be trying to make business travel sound less businessy or something.

She glanced at the numbers on a shop window to get her bearings and calculated that the hotel was another eight blocks down, toward the lake. She hadn't been to Tahoe since college, she realized as she drove, smiling at the shops boasting kites and artwork and jewelry and clothes. In the winter, there would be skis lined up everywhere, but during the summer, there were water toys and rafts instead. People dotted the streets in their bright summer colors and sunglasses, lolling at café tables and sauntering in and out of stores. The weather was perfect for being outdoors, the air kissed with just a hint of the cool breeze gliding off the lake, the sky a faultless blue streaked with gauzy clouds.

Kendall smiled at the promise inherent in the day. It was a good omen. She had been right to leave Matthias's employ. Stephen DeGallo's offer couldn't have come at a better time. Funny how things just worked out perfectly sometimes. She had a full week to spend in one of the most beautiful places on earth, learning about a new career that, she hoped, would be hers for the rest of her life. Her future at OmniTech was wide-open. If she worked hard and did everything right—who knew?—she might even become the CEO of the company herself someday. Stephen DeGallo was a confirmed bachelor in his late forties with no family he was bringing up through the ranks, and he was known for rewarding his workers with generous benefits and bonuses. Even if he never groomed Kendall for his own position at the company, there was every reason to believe he might someday install her as the head of one of the scores of businesses he owned. Unlike Matthias, who had never offered any indication that he would ever consider Kendall for anything more than his assist—

Dammit. She was thinking about him again.

She pushed Matthias out of her brain—again—and looked for another street number. Two more blocks.

When she braked for a red light, she used the opportunity to get her bearings. A glance at her watch told her it was just coming up on three o'clock, precisely the time she'd anticipated arriving, knowing her room would be ready by then. She was supposed to meet Stephen and the other trainees at six for an informal dinner, so they could all get to know one another, and training officially began at eight in the morning. Dress would be casual, but Kendall had packed a couple of suits in with her trousers and shirts, just in case. She was, after all, a consummate professional.

Of course, she was in Lake Tahoe, too, so she'd also included blue jeans and T-shirts and shorts and sandals, her preferred attire for relaxing. She wasn't such a workaholic that she didn't take advantage of her off time. Unlike Matthias, who—

Dammit, she was doing it again.

The light changed green, so she banished thoughts of Matthias—*again*—and urged the accelerator down lightly, taking the last two blocks slowly. The lake was in view now, but she didn't see any hotels large enough to qualify for corporate lodgings up ahead. She took her eyes off the road long enough to glance down at the passenger seat, where she'd laid the directions and a map, to confirm she had the address right. Maybe she'd written it down wrong, she thought. Because this block and the one beyond it was nothing but more quaint shops and cafés and cozy B and Bs.

Just as she neared the end of the last block and began to look for a place to turn around, she saw a sign with an arrow pointing to the right that read Parking for Timber Lake Inn. Braking quickly, she was able to make the turn just in time.

But the drive led to the entrance of a tidy, cheerful little bed-and-breakfast. Kendall frowned, wondering where she'd gone wrong, then noted a sign above the door that identified it as the very hotel she'd been looking for. Huh. That was odd. The place looked more like a honeymoon hotel than it did a corporate facility. Stephen DeGallo must like to use places like this to make his new hires feel more comfortable. Yet another way in which he differed from Matthias, who, Kendall was sure, would have scheduled an orientation for…

Well, actually, Matthias would have trained people in the buildings where they would be working, she thought. Or rather, he'd have *other* people training his new employees in the buildings where they would be working. It would be more professional that way. More businesslike. God forbid he should ever want anyone to feel any other way.

When Kendall realized she was thinking about Matthias *again,* she shoved the thought away *again*—harder this time—and pushed open the car door. By now a bellman had emerged from the hotel and was descending the stairs to help her with her bag. Instead of the liveried uniform he might have worn at a larger hotel, however, he was dressed in khaki shorts and a polo bearing the logo of the Timber Lake Inn stitched on the breast pocket. Coupled with his shaggy blond hair and ruddy complexion, he looked as if he should be standing at the edge of the ocean toting a surfboard instead of lugging bags for a lakeside hotel.

"Dude," he greeted her with a smile, reinforcing the image. "Welcome to the Timber Lake Inn. I'm Sean. I'll get your bags."

"Thanks," Kendall replied with a smile of her own as she reached into the car to pop the trunk open. "I'm Kendall Scarborough. I'm here for the OmniTech orientation session."

Sean nodded. "Well, wherever that's going on, you can probably get there by walking. We're pretty centrally located here."

The comment puzzled Kendall. "It's going on here," she said. "At the hotel."

Sean's eyebrows shot up at that. "Whoa. First I've heard about it. But then, I was on vacation last week and just got back today. All I knew about going on this week was the Tyson-Gerhart wedding and the Truckee Ski Club reunion. Those have got us booked to full capacity."

Kendall looked at the hotel again. It didn't look big enough to host those functions and a training session. Not that she'd expected the OmniTech orientation to be a huge event, but since it would run for a week, and since Stephen DeGallo himself would be part of it, she'd just assumed the company would be training quite a few people. A business that size employed hundreds in San Francisco alone, and Kendall had been under the impression that this session would include new hires from all over the Northwest. There must be more to the hotel than the two stories she could see.

Sean collected her bags and she followed him into the lobby, which immediately made her feel comfortable. It was everything a place called the Timber Lake Inn should be, from its knotty pine walls to the huge creek stone fireplace on the opposite side of the room. The hardwood floors were covered here and there by woven rugs in Native American geometrics, and wrought iron fixtures hung from the exposed log ceiling. A wide staircase to the right of the reception desk led up to a line of rooms on the second floor, but none of them seemed to be meeting rooms. As if to illustrate that, one of the doors opened and a couple exited, looping their arms around each other and cuddling like newlyweds.

Nothing about the place suggested it was used for business events. In fact, the place looked…well, cozy. That was the only word that came to Kendall's mind.

The word returned when she entered her room…until she discovered it was actually a suite appointed with more pine walls and more exposed ceiling beams and more Native American rugs. In the main room, French doors opened onto a spacious balcony that offered a glorious view of the lake, which was picked up again in the bedroom by a broad picture window. The bathroom boasted a jacuzzi and small television, and there was a wet bar tucked into the far side of the living room. An enormous basket of fresh fruit and wine sat at the center of the dining table, and a massive bouquet of flowers, fragrant and splashy, was perched on the desk. Envelopes bearing her name—her *first* name—were tucked into each.

"Still think DeGallo wants you only for your MBA and your business savvy?"

Kendall spun around with a start at the question to find Matthias leaning in the still-open door to her room. Her lips parted in surprise, but not entirely because of his unexpected arrival. He looked…different. And not just because he was casually dressed in clay-colored trousers and a navy-blue polo, where she was more accustomed to seeing him in suits. She'd seen him dressed for non-business-related functions before, everything from rugby in the park to black-tie opening nights. It wasn't Matthias's clothing that looked off today. It was Matthias.

His clothes were a little wrinkled, his hair was a little shaggy, and his eyes were a little shadowed, as if he wasn't getting quite enough sleep. In fact, his whole face looked a little shadowed, a little leaner, a little rougher. And Matthias had never been "a little" anything. He was an all-or-nothing kind of man, emphasis on the *all*, especially where his physical appearance went.

She ignored the little pang of concern that pinched her at seeing him in his less-tidy-than-usual state. It was none of her business if he was working too much. None of her business if whoever he'd hired to take her place wasn't keeping him on track the way she had. She wasn't her boss's keeper. Especially since Matthias wasn't even her boss anymore.

"What are you doing here?" she asked by way of a

greeting, congratulating herself on keeping her voice steady, clear and indifferent. "I mean, I know why you're in Tahoe. But what are you doing *here?* At my hotel?"

He raised a shoulder and let it drop, then pushed himself away from the doorjamb. As he strode into the room, he told her, "I made better time driving from San Francisco than I thought I would, so I'm a little ahead of schedule. I don't have to meet the caretaker for another hour, so I thought I'd drop in and say hello."

Kendall eyed him suspiciously. It wasn't like Matthias to "drop in" on anyone, for any reason. And he must have gone to some lengths to find out where she would be staying and when she would be arriving, because she hadn't shared any of that information with him. Not to mention they hadn't exactly parted on the best of terms. They hadn't spoken to or seen each other since he'd had her escorted out of the building like a common thief. If he was here now, it had to be because he wanted something.

So she asked him, "What do you want?"

Matthias looked at Kendall and wondered which of dozens of answers to that question he should give her. He wanted a lot of things, actually. He wanted the Perkins contract. He wanted the Barton Limited stock to go through the roof. He wanted to be worth a billion dollars by the time he was forty. Hell, he even wanted world peace, since it would create so many new business-friendly governments. And, okay, he wanted a new personal assistant, too, since, so far, everyone he'd interviewed had been, at best, unqualified and, at worst, a lobotomy gone tragically wrong.

Mostly, though, he wanted Kendall to open her eyes and see what was so obvious to him. Talk about a lobotomy. What had happened to the pragmatic, professional, enterprising, efficient woman he'd hired? Looking at Kendall now...

Well, actually, looking at Kendall now, Matthias wondered what she'd done to herself. The dark blond hair she normally had twisted up out of her way hung loose, cascading past her shoulders in a thick, silky mass. Wow, it was a lot longer than he'd thought—not that he'd ever thought much about Kendall's hair. But it was long. Thick. Silky. Had he mentioned silky? And long? And thick? Her glasses were gone, too, and he noted with some surprise that her eyes were huge without them. And green. He'd never noticed that Kendall had green eyes. Really green eyes. Pale green. Like bottle glass. And every bit as clear.

"What do you want, Mr. Barton?" she asked again, bringing his thoughts back to where they needed to be.

It was a good question, he thought. He wished he had a good answer to go with it. But the fact was, he still wasn't sure why he was here. Yeah, her hotel was on his way, but even if it hadn't been, he would have driven the extra miles to see her. He'd done a little checking this week—okay, he'd done a lot of snooping—to find out where Kendall would be staying and the particulars of this "week-long orientation." But his mole at OmniTech—yes, Matthias had one there, just as he was sure DeGallo had one at Barton Limited—hadn't been able to uncover much about it.

Which had just hammered home to Matthias that the guy was up to no good. Had there been a legitimate orientation seminar going on, it would have been a matter of company record. As far as Matthias could tell, however, Kendall was the only new hire of any consequence that Stephen DeGallo had made recently. As he'd told her two weeks ago, the guy didn't hire outside the company for the kind of position he'd offered her. And any alleged orientation there might have been for her position should have taken place on-site—not in a cozy, romantic little hotel overlooking Lake Tahoe.

"I've come to offer you your job back," he said, surprising himself as much as he'd obviously surprised Kendall. He really hadn't been intending to do that at all when he drove into town. He'd just been planning to…

Okay, he wasn't exactly sure what he'd been planning to do. But now that he thought more about it, offering Kendall her job back made sense. No one he'd interviewed had come close to matching her qualifications. Matthias was confident that if he made her the right offer, she'd come back on board. Everyone had their price. Kendall was no exception. She'd just been feeling unappreciated, he told himself. He hadn't emphasized enough how valuable she was to Barton Limited. Oh, sure, he'd given her raises and more benefits. But any good employee needed ego stroking, too. Just because Kendall had never seemed like the kind of person who wanted that kind of thing didn't mean it wasn't important to her.

He didn't know why he hadn't thought about that before. At least not consciously. Evidently his brain *had* been considering it *sub*consciously, to have thrown out the offer to hire her back. That was probably what had been behind Matthias's driving into town to find her in the first place. He'd been planning—subconsciously—to renegotiate the terms of her employment and invite her back.

Yeah, that was it. It had to be. Why else would he have come?

Kendall, however, didn't seem to be as open to the idea of her return to Barton Limited as Matthias was, because she didn't answer him right away. In fact, she was looking at him as if she was kind of indignant.

No, it must be grateful, he told himself immediately. Indignity, gratitude…those got mixed up all the time. They had a lot of the same letters in common. After all, why would she feel indignant?

"I have a job," she said tersely.

Or maybe she'd said it sweetly. Those got mixed up a lot, too. Matthias was sure of it. The letter thing again.

"And I'm very excited about it," she added.

No, definitely terse, he thought. And not a little shirty.

Instead of replying, he strode across the room to the broad panoramic windows that looked out over the crystalline blue water of the lake and the bright blue sky above it. The day was glorious, the view crisp and clean, the dark green mountains on the other side of the water streaked with purple shadows from the forests of trees, the sun dappling the water as if it were scattering diamonds. This place was as far removed from the skyscrapers and concrete of San Francisco as it could be, and the last thing anyone should think about here was work. Which was why Matthias so seldom visited places like this. And which was why—one of many *whys*—he knew Stephen DeGallo was up to no good.

He sensed more than heard Kendall as she came up behind him, and was unprepared for the feeling that washed over him when she came to a halt behind him. He'd been edgy since leaving San Francisco, as he always was when he traveled. Travel was such a waste of time, and Matthias was always impatient getting from point A to point B so he could get on with business. This time, however, the feeling hadn't lessened once he'd arrived at his destination.

He'd still been feeling anxious when he entered Kendall's room. But when she stood beside him then, he was suddenly overcome by a feeling of calmness. Peacefulness. A strange sense of well-being that he hadn't felt for…

Well, a couple of weeks, anyway.

She said nothing as she gazed out the window, only studied the same view Matthias was considering himself. But he knew there must be some part of her brain that was questioning DeGallo's motives by now. She was a smart woman. She had good instincts. It was what made her so good at what she did.

"Look at that view," he said anyway, trivializing with a cliché what was a staggeringly beautiful piece of work. "You don't see views like that in the city." He turned to face Kendall before adding meaningfully, "Where most job orientations take place."

She slumped a little at the comment, expelling a tired-sounding sigh. But she said nothing to deny his more-than-obvious allegation.

"And look at this room," he said further, turning again and sweeping both arms open. "Who gets a place like this when they're undergoing orientation for a new job?"

Kendall sighed again, still sounding weary, but turned her body in the same direction as his. "New vice presidents for the company," she told him. "That's who. Stephen just wants to make a good impression, that's all."

Matthias dipped his head in concession, however small, to that. Then he strode to the table where there sat a bouquet of flowers more massive than *any* man *any*where had ever sent to *any* woman for *any* reason—be it declaring his love or groveling for forgiveness. He plucked the card from a particularly luscious-looking bloom and began to open it.

"Matthias, don't—" Kendall began.

He halted, snapping his head up at that, not because she had told him to stop, but because she had addressed him by his first name. Never, not once, during the five years she'd worked for him had she called him Matthias. Because never, not once, had he given her the okay to do it. And the fact that she had stepped over that line now so thoroughly, without his permission...

Hmm. Actually, now that he'd heard her call him Matthias, he realized he kind of liked the way his name sounded coming from her lips. In fact, he kind of liked the way her lips looked right now, having just said his name. Parted softly in surprise, and maybe embarrassment, as if she hadn't intended to call him Matthias, and now she wasn't sure what to do to take it back, or if she even wanted to take it back. What was strange was that Matthias didn't want her to take it back. In fact, he wanted her to say it again. Even more surprising, he realized the context in which he wanted to hear her say his name had nothing to do with her job, and everything to do with, well, other reasons people came to Lake Tahoe.

"Don't," she said again, more softly this time. Omitting the use of his name.

This time, too, she extended her hand toward the small envelope he still held tucked between his index and middle fingers. Not sure why he did it, Matthias pulled his hand toward himself, out of her reach. She took another step forward, bringing her body to within touching distance of his, then hesitated. But she didn't drop her hand, and for a moment, he thought—hoped—she would trail her hand after his to retrieve the card. He even found himself looking forward to her fingers tangling with his as they vied for possession. And although it was clear she was grappling with the possibility of that very thing herself—or maybe because she was grappling with it—she dropped her hand to her side again, ceding to him with clear reluctance.

The victory was strangely hollow, but Matthias shouldered it anyway. Opening the envelope, he withdrew the card, then scanned the sentiment upon it. He wasn't sure if it was DeGallo's writing, but it was masculine and forceful, and he suspected DeGallo himself had indeed penned the words. The task hadn't been left to an assistant to complete, which was what Matthias would have done in the same situation.

Then again, Matthias would never have been in this situation. Oh, he might have wooed someone away from one of his competitors specifically to learn more about that competitor's practices, but he would have been straightforward about it. He wouldn't have set up the new hire in a honeymoon suite with a breathtaking view of a romantic environment and called it orientation. And he wouldn't have sent flowers—with *any*one's signature.

He shook his head as he read aloud the sentiment DeGallo had written. "Kendall," he said, "Can't wait to have you navigating our PR waters. Welcome aboard!" He looked up at Kendall then, but she was staring at the wall. "Navigating our PR waters?" he repeated. "Was that the best he could do?"

Now Kendall turned to look at Matthias, her huge, clear green eyes penetrating deep enough to heat something in his chest. "Well, there *is* a lake out there," she said lamely. "Besides, what would *you* have said to welcome a new employee?"

"I would have said, 'Get to work,'" he replied. "And I would have said it to that new employee's face. I wouldn't go through all this ridiculous pretense to make her feel like she was more important than she actually is."

Two bright spots of color flared on Kendall's cheeks at that. She nodded brusquely. "Of course you wouldn't," she said. "Because no one is important to you. You think the success of Barton Limited is because of you and you alone. You have no appreciation for how many people it takes to make a company prosper, and you have no clue how to take care of the ones who are doing the best work. And if you're not careful, then—"

She halted abruptly, her eyes widening in what he could only guess was horror that she'd just leaped like a gazelle across the line she had previously only overstepped. Matthias narrowed his eyes at her, his own lips parting now in surprise. Kendall had never challenged him like this before. Hell, challenged? he asked himself. Compared to her usual self-containment, she'd just read him the riot act. With a bullhorn. Sure, she'd taken exception in the past to some of his decisions—okay, edicts—but she'd always pointed out her concerns with discretion. And deference. But this reaction was completely unlike her. Totally unexpected. And extremely…

Matthias stopped himself before allowing the impression to fully form. Because the impression had nothing to do with his reaction to Kendall as an employee, and everything to do with his reaction to her as a…a person.

"Is that what you really think?" he asked, deciding to focus on that instead of…the other thing.

She hesitated only a second, then nodded. And then, a little less forcefully than she'd spoken before, she added, "Yes. Sir." And then, a little more forcefully, she altered her response to, "Yes. Matthias."

There it was again, he marveled. That ripple of heat that should have been disapproval of her familiarity by using his first name, but which was instead…something else. Something he told himself to try to figure out later, because he really needed to respond to Kendall's allegation that he was so self-centered. But because of the way she was looking at him, all clear-green-eyed and hot-pink-cheeked and tumbling-silky-haired, all he could manage in response was, "Oh, really?"

A moment passed in which neither of them spoke, or moved, or even breathed. Then Kendall's lips turned up almost imperceptibly, into a smile with what only someone who had the vast experience Matthias had with the emotion could identify.

Victory.

Kendall Scarborough had it in her head that she'd just won whatever the two of them had been engaged in. Now if Matthias could just figure out what the two of them had just engaged in, maybe he'd know what to do next.

Kendall, however, didn't seem to be having the same problem he had. Because she settled her hands on her hips in a way that was at once relaxed and challenging, and she asked again, "Was there some reason you came here this afternoon, Matthias? Is there something you wanted?"

He honestly had no idea how to answer her. Because for the first time in his life, Matthias didn't know what he wanted. He was too off-kilter looking at Kendall and thinking about Kendall and listening to Kendall saying his name and marveling at how Kendall had thrown him so off-kilter.

But he didn't want to look foolish, either—that would have been another first he would have just as soon done without. So he reached into his trouser pocket and removed a small gadget he'd purchased for himself the day after she'd left his employ. Something called a… Well, he couldn't remember what it was called now, but it was supposed to be even better than the… Whatever that other thing was he used to use for keeping track of his appointments and obligations.

Then he held it out to Kendall and replied, "Yeah. Do you have any idea how this thing works? I keep getting e-mail from some deposed prince in Nigeria who needs my help freeing up some frozen assets he's trying to get out of the country, and I'd really like to help him out, because he promised me a more than generous share once he's fluid again. Plus, this woman named Trixie just got a new Web cam she wants to show me, and I'm thinking it might be technology I'd like to invest in."

He looked at Kendall, who was looking back at him as if he'd just grown a second head. "What?" he said.

She crossed the room in a half-dozen long strides and opened the door. Then she pointed to the hallway beyond with one finger. "Out," she said. "Now."

His mouth dropped open in surprise. "What, you're not going to help me?"

"I'm not your assistant anymore, Matthias."

Oh, as if he needed reminding of *that*. "But—"

"Out," she repeated. "Now."

He shook his head in disbelief. But he did as she asked him to. Told him to. Demanded he do. The door was slamming shut behind him before he'd even cleared it, missing his backside by *that* much. He spun around, and went so far as to lift a fist to pound on it again. But he stopped himself before completing the action.

There was a better way to go about this, he told himself.

He just had to figure out what it was. Because Kendall *was* making a mistake, thinking OmniTech was the place she needed to be. Where she needed to be was with him. Or, rather, with Barton Limited, he quickly corrected himself. Now all he had to do was figure out a way to make her realize that, too.

Three

Kendall leaned back against the door through which Matthias had just exited and tried to get a handle on everything that had just happened.

She'd thrown him out, she marveled. She'd looked at the BlackBerry in his hand, incredulous that, just when they were starting to have an exchange that felt evenly matched, he would ask her to program the little gizmo the way she had so many others when he was paying her to be his underling, and then she'd asked—no, *told*—him to leave. Even more stunning than that was the fact that Matthias had done as she asked—no, *told*—him to and had left. Without a word of argument. Without a word of exception. Without a word of reproach.

Okay, and without a word of farewell, either.

The point was that Kendall had taken charge of a situation with Matthias and she had mastered it. Eventually. Just because there had been a few moments in between that had been filled with strange bits of weirdness didn't diminish the enormity of that achievement.

But just *what,* exactly, had that weirdness been about? she asked herself now. There had been times during their conversation when Matthias had looked at her almost as if he were seeing someone else, someone he didn't quite know, someone with whom he wasn't entirely comfortable. Someone he wasn't sure he liked. It had been…weird. And her response had been weird, too. She'd suddenly been aware of him in a way she hadn't been when she'd worked for him. Or, at least, in a way she hadn't allowed herself to think about when she worked for him.

She let herself think about it now.

The day Matthias had announced his engagement to Lauren Conover, Kendall had experienced a reaction that had surprised her. A lot. And she'd realized that day that her feelings for her boss might perhaps, possibly, conceivably go a little beyond professional. Because where she had never minded the other women who came and went in Matthias's life—because they always came and went—when he'd made a move to join himself permanently to someone else, Kendall had felt a little…

Well, weird.

At first, she'd told herself it was just disappointment that such a smart man would do something as stupid as arrange a marriage of convenience for himself. Then she'd told herself what she felt was annoyance that, because of his engagement, he wanted her to arrange so many events for him that had nothing to do with work. In fact, she'd run through a veritable grocery list of feelings in response to

Matthias's announced nuptials: denial, then anger, then bargaining, then depression…

Hang on a minute, Kendall thought now. Those were the stages of grief. And no way had she felt *that*. No way had she been *that* far gone on her boss.

Ultimately, however, she had been forced to admit the truth. That maybe, perhaps, possibly, conceivably, she had developed…feelings… for her employer. Feelings of attachment. Feelings of allegiance. Feelings of… She closed her eyes tight and made herself admit it. Feelings of…affection.

The recognition that she had begun to feel things for her boss that she had no business feeling—even her allegiance wasn't for things that related to work—was what had cemented her conviction that she would, once and for all, tender her resignation. Even after his engagement to Lauren was canceled, she'd known she had to go. She couldn't risk falling for Matthias, because he would never care for her in any way other than the professional. He didn't care about anyone in any way other than the professional. That the offer from Stephen DeGallo had come on the heels of the cancellation of Matthias's wedding had just been an exclamation point to punctuate the obvious. She had done the right thing by leaving Matthias. Or, rather, she hastily corrected herself, by leaving Matthias's employ.

She just hoped taking the job with Stephen DeGallo had been the right thing to do, too.

Some lodge, Matthias thought as he pulled into the drive of what looked more like a boutique hotel than a private residence. Had it not been for the fact that he'd been here once before—three months ago, when his brother, Luke, was in residence—he wouldn't have been sure he was in the right place. He turned off the ignition and exited the car, hauled his leather weekender out of the backseat and made his way to the entrance where the caretaker was waiting for him.

The woman was dressed in a pale yellow straight skirt and a white sleeveless top, a canvas gimme cap decorated with a logo he didn't recognize pulled low on her forehead. Coupled with her sunglasses, it was hard to tell what she looked like, but what he could see was pretty, in a wholesome kind of way. The ponytail hanging out of the cap's opening was streaked dark blond, and she had some decent curves, so it wasn't surprising that Matthias found himself comparing her to Kendall…and thinking how nice it would be if it was Kendall who was here to greet him instead. Not because he wanted to spend a month here with Kendall, of course, but because if Kendall was here, he could get a lot more work done, that was all.

"I assume you're Mary?" he asked the woman by way of a greeting. "I'm sorry I'm late."

She seemed to deflate a little when she got a good look at him, and only then did he realize she had seemed kind of expectant as he strode up the walk. Maybe she'd thought he was someone else, since his own appearance probably wasn't easy to discern, either, thanks to his own sunglasses.

She nodded. "I'm the caretaker." Without further ado, she extended a key that dangled from a rather elaborate key chain and added, "Here's the key. Just leave it on the kitchen table at the end of the month. I've stocked the refrigerator and cabinets, and there's some carryout from a local takeaway gourmet. But if it's not to your taste or you'd like something specific, there are menus for some restaurants in Hunter's Landing on top of the fridge. I can recommend Clearwater's and the Lakeside Diner for sure. Or if you do the cooking thing, there's a market just east of where you turned off to find the lodge."

Her voice was soft but dispassionate, and she spoke as if she were reading from a script. And not very dramatically, at that. "Tahoe City is about a half hour north, the Nevada state line about twenty minutes east. If you want to gamble," she added, as if wanting to clarify.

"Not like that," Matthias told her. When he gambled, he liked for the stakes to be much higher than mere cash.

Mary nodded. "Would you like for me to show you around the place? Explain how everything works?"

"I assume it's all pretty standard," he replied. Not to mention he had no intention of seeing how anything worked. That way lay madness.

"Standard, yes," Mary told him. "But there are quite a few amenities. Hot tub, Jacuzzi, gourmet kitchen, plasma TV…"

He held up a hand to stop her. He wasn't the type to indulge in any of those things. He had too much work to do. "It won't be necessary," he told her. "Thanks, anyway."

"Then, if you won't be needing anything else?" she asked.

Well, there was nothing he needed that she could provide, anyway, he thought. So he told her, "Nothing, thanks."

"Emergency numbers are on the fridge, too," she said. "Including mine. Hopefully you won't need them, either."

She hesitated before leaving, studying Matthias's face for a moment as if she were looking for something. Then, suddenly, she said, "Goodbye," and turned to walk down the front steps. For the merest, most nebulous second, she seemed a little familiar somehow. He didn't know if it was her walk, her voice, the way she carried herself or what, but there was…something about her that reminded him so much of someone else. He just couldn't quite put his finger on who.

And then the impression was gone, as quickly as it had materialized. Mary was gone, too, having climbed back into her car and backed it out of the driveway. Matthias jingled the key in his hand absently, shrugged off his odd ruminations and turned to unlock the front door, closing it behind himself once he was inside. Out of habit, he tossed his battered leather weekender—the one he'd traveled with since college—onto the nearest piece of furniture. No small feat, that, since the place was huge, with a foyer the size of a Giants dugout, and the nearest piece of furniture was half a stadium away. He didn't care if he knocked something over in the process. He was still pissed off at Hunter for making all of them rearrange their lives for a month to come here and do whatever the hell it was they were supposed to do.

But then, he was still pissed off at Hunter for dying, too.

Of course, if he were honest with himself, Matthias would have to admit that he was more pissed off at himself than anyone else. He hadn't meant to lose touch with the Seven Samurai over the years. It had just…happened. Time happened. Distance happened. Work happened. Life happened. People grew up. They grew apart. They went their separate ways. Happened all the time. He and Hunter and the rest of them had all been kids when they'd made pacts and promises to stay friends forever. Hell, Matthias hadn't even kept in touch with his own brother. Then again, when your brother did things like accusing you of cheating him in business and stealing your fiancée, it was understandable why you'd allow for some distance.

As soon as the thought formed in his head, Matthias pushed it away. He was being unfair to Luke. Really unfair this time, and not the phony-baloney unfairness of which his brother had always accused him. Their father hadn't exactly been a proponent of fairness, anyway. He had pitted the two of them against each other from the day the twins were old enough to compete. Which, to the old man's way of thinking, had been within seconds of their emerging from the womb. If there had been some way to make the boys vie for something against each other, Samuel Sullivan Barton found a way to do it. Who could win the most merit badges in Cub Scouts. Who could sell the most wrapping paper for the school fund-raiser. Who could score the most baskets, make the most touchdowns, pitch the best game. As children, they'd been more like rivals than brothers.

It had only gotten worse after their father's death and the terms of his will had been made public. Samuel had decreed that whichever of the boys made a million dollars first, the estate would go to him in its entirety. Matthias had won. Though winning had been relative. Luke had accused him, unjustly, of cheating and hadn't spoken to him for years. It hadn't been until recently that the two men had shared anything. And then what they'd shared was Lauren Conover, the woman who'd agreed to be Matthias's wife. It had been the ultimate competition for Luke…until he'd fallen in love with the prize. And although Matthias had come to terms with what had happened, things between him and his brother still weren't exactly smooth. Or simple. Or settled.

Man, what was it about peoples' last wills and testaments that they always sent Matthias's life in a new direction?

He sighed as he leaned against the front door and drove

his gaze around the lodge. In college, they'd said they wanted to build a cabin. But "cabin" evoked an image of a rustic, no-frills, crowded little shack in the woods with few amenities and even fewer comforts. This place was like something from *Citizen Kane,* had the movie been filmed in Technicolor. The great room ceiling soared up two stories, with expansive windows running the entire length of one wall, offering an incredible view of the lake. The pine paneling was polished to a honeyed sheen, the wide planked floors buffed to a satin finish. At one end of the room was a fireplace big enough to host the United Arab Emirates, a sofa and chairs clustered before it that, ironically, invited an intimate gathering of friends.

The place was exactly the sort of retreat Matthias would have expected Hunter to have. Handsomely furnished. Blissfully quiet. Generously outfitted. And yet there was something missing that prevented it from being completely comfortable. Something that Hunter had obviously forgotten to include, but Matthias couldn't quite put his finger on what.

He pushed himself away from the door and made his way to where his weekender had landed—just shy of actually hitting the nearest piece of furniture he'd been aiming for. His footsteps echoed hollowly on the hardwood floor as he went, an auditory reminder of just how alone he would be while he was here. Matthias wasn't used to traveling alone. Kendall had always come with him on business trips, and even though they'd naturally had separate quarters, he'd seen her virtually from sunup to sundown. Of course, this wasn't, technically, a business trip. But he would have brought Kendall along, had she still been in his employ, because he would be working while he was here. And Kendall had been a big part of his work for five years.

Five years, he thought as he grabbed his bag and strode toward the stairs that led up to the second floor. In the scheme of things, it wasn't such a long time. But it comprised the entirety of Kendall's work life. He was the only employer she'd had since graduating. He'd been her first. Her only. He'd been the one who had introduced her to the ways of business, the one who'd taught her how to achieve the most satisfaction in what she did, the one who'd shown her which positions to take on things that would yield the most pleasurable results. And now, after he'd been the one to initiate her in all the intricacies of the working relationship, another employer had wooed her away.

"Oh, for God's sake, Barton," he muttered to himself as he climbed the stairs. "You're talking about her like she's an old lover."

He waited for the laughter that was bound to come from entertaining a thought like that, but for some reason, it didn't come. Instead, he was overcome by a strange kind of fatigue that made him want to blow off work for the rest of the day and instead go do something more—

The thought made him stop dead in his tracks, halfway up the stairs. Blow off work? Since when had he *ever* blown off work? For any reason? And how could anything be *more* than work? Work was everything. Talk about something that should have made him erupt into laughter.

But he didn't laugh at that, either. Instead, he realized he'd left his laptop out in the trunk of the car. Worse, he realized that, even if he'd remembered to bring it in with him, he wasn't completely sure how to get to all the files he needed to get to. That had always been Kendall's job. Knowing how to pull up whatever needed pulling up and pulling it up for him. Hell, half the time, she'd taken care of whatever needed pulling and then pushed it back down again.

He was going to have to hire a temp for now, he told himself. Surely there was a temp agency close by. Tahoe City maybe. Too bad Kendall wasn't here. She would have found just the right person, and she would have had the person here five minutes ago. But how hard could it be? he asked himself. He just needed to find the phone book, and he'd be good to go.

So where did people keep their phone books, anyway…

By the time she entered the bar of the Timber Lake Inn that evening, Kendall had accepted the fact that it, like everything else in the establishment, would be cozy. Sure enough, it was. Like the rest of the hotel, it was pine-paneled with hardwood floors and Native American rugs, but the lighting was lower than in the other public rooms, softer and more golden, and very… Well, there was just no way around it. Romantic.

Matthias was right. This wasn't the sort of hotel any businessman in his right mind would use for business functions. Nevertheless, she was confident Stephen DeGallo had his reasons for using it. *Besides* trying to lull Kendall into a false sense of security, which Matthias had implied—hah—was the case. Or to lull her into anything else, either. For all she knew, the Timber Lake Inn was the only hotel in Lake Tahoe that had had any openings when Stephen scheduled the orientation. And the fact that Lake Tahoe itself was such a cozy, romantic destination that was kind of an odd choice for a business orientation had nothing to do with anything. It was centrally located, that was all.

She shook the thought almost literally out of her head

and smoothed her hand one final time over the chocolate-brown trousers and cream-colored shirt she'd donned for the evening. Stephen had said the evening would be casual, and what she had on was casual attire. It *was*. Even if it was the same kind of thing she'd worn to work every day when she was with Matthias. Ah, *working for* Matthias, she quickly corrected herself. And the reason she'd wound her hair up into its usual workplace bun and put on her usual workplace glasses wasn't because she was trying to overcompensate for the cozy, romantic environment. It *wasn't*. It was because she just hadn't felt like going to any trouble. She had low-maintenance hair. So sue her. And even though she didn't need her glasses all the time, what with the low lighting and everything, she figured she'd need them.

So there.

She scanned the bar for a group of people who looked as if they were training for new careers, but saw only couples at a handful of tables here and there. Cozy couples. Romantic couples. In fact, one couple was being *so* romantic Kendall wanted to yell, "Jeez, people, get a room!" Glancing down at her watch, she realized she was a little early, so maybe she was the first member of the OmniTech orientation group to arrive. Then a movement in the corner of the room—the *farthest* corner—and the *darkest* corner, she couldn't help noticing—caught her eye, and she realized it was Stephen DeGallo, waving at her.

She lifted a hand in return and made her way in that direction, picking her way through the tables as she looked around for anyone else who might be joining him. And somehow, she refrained from muttering, *Jeez, people, get a room* as she passed by the overly demonstrative couple.

Nor did she toss a glass of ice water over them, which was another thought she hadn't quite been able to quell.

"Kendall," Stephen said warmly when she was within earshot. "Great to see you again. Glad you made it in one piece."

"It's great to be here, Stephen," she said as she extended her hand in greeting. "Thanks again for giving me this opportunity. I'm very excited about working for OmniTech."

He grasped her hand in both of his, not really shaking it, per se, just holding it for perhaps a moment longer than was necessary, something that made her think about Matthias's warning again. Which she immediately pushed out of her brain. Stephen was just being friendly. And she was just being overly sensitive, thanks to Matthias's ridiculous ideas about Stephen only wanting her because of her ties to Barton Limited. This was what happened when you were employed by a workaholic for so many years. You forgot that normal people could be casual and friendly, even in professional situations.

And Stephen's smile did put Kendall immediately at ease. Although he wasn't a handsome man, he was by no means unattractive. He was slim and fit, and was dressed according to his own edict—casually—in a pair of softly faded blue jeans and a white polo shirt. His blue eyes held intelligence and good humor, and his dark blond hair was just beginning to go gray, threaded here and there with bits of silver. What he lacked in handsomeness, he more than made up for in charisma. He was just one of those people who had a gift for taking charge of a situation without being overbearing, and making people feel better that he had.

Kendall had done her homework after his offer of employment, so she knew quite a bit about him. In many ways, he was as devoted to his company as Matthias was to Barton Limited, but where Matthias's extracurricular and social activities all still seemed to involve his work, Stephen DeGallo was a man who enjoyed his leisure time. He was a champion yachtsman and active in a charitable foundation he had started ten years ago that mentored gifted, but underprivileged high school students.

He was not just a good businessman, but a good guy, Kendall had discovered. And her admiration of him was due to both.

She seated herself in the chair he held out for her, folding her elbows on the table and weaving her fingers lightly together. Then she gave him her most businesslike smile. "Am I the first to arrive?" she asked, even though the answer was obvious.

"Actually," Stephen said as he folded himself into the chair opposite hers, "right now, you're the *only* one who's here."

Kendall told herself she just imagined the note of vague discomfort she thought she heard in his voice. More of Matthias's influence on her nerves, she was sure. Still, it was odd that no one else had arrived yet.

"Don't tell me I'm the only one who got here on time," she said.

"No, of course not," he told her. "The others just aren't scheduled to arrive until Wednesday."

Wednesday? Kendall thought. That was two whole days away. "Oh," she said, the word sounding more disappointed than she'd intended.

"The others are training for management positions," he said by way of an explanation. "You're the only VP candidate this time around. So I thought it would be nice if the two of us could have a couple of days where I could go over some of the policies and procedures that won't be pertinent to everyone else's training."

That made sense, Kendall thought.

"But first, a drink," he said, motioning to a waiter who had been hovering within range. "What would you like? I discovered a wonderful California pinot noir recently that's absolutely delightful."

"Thanks," Kendall told him, "but I'll just have a bottle of sparkling water."

He threw her a look of mock effrontery. "But we're celebrating your joining the OmniTech team," he objected.

"Which is why I ordered *sparkling* water," she said with a smile.

He smiled back, dipping his head forward in acknowledgment. "Then I'll have the same," he told the waiter. "Now then," he added as their server departed, "I thought we could spend much of tonight talking about how—"

"Stephen DeGallo!"

Kendall flinched at the sound of the booming, all-too-familiar voice, but managed to otherwise keep her irritation in check. Well, enough that no one would notice it, anyway. Though she had to admit that Stephen didn't look any happier about the interruption than she was. Nevertheless, good businessman—and guy—that he was, he smiled as he rose to greet Matthias. Kendall turned in her chair to acknowledge her former employer, but remained seated, hoping that small act of discourtesy would illustrate her pique in a way that wasn't quite as impolite as other actions might have been. Actions like, oh…Kendall didn't know. Tripping him as he strode past her to shake Stephen's hand. Calling him a big poophead. Stuff like that.

She noticed Stephen didn't grasp Matthias's hand in

both of his the way he had hers—in fact, he gave Matthias's one, two, three firm, manly shakes and released it. Then again, Matthias was a rival, so naturally, Stephen's greeting to him wouldn't be as familiar as his to Kendall had been. Similarly, it was understandable why Stephen's posture, too, with Matthias would be more assertive, more straightforward, more businesslike, than it had been with Kendall. Wouldn't it?

Yeah. Sure. Of course.

"Matthias Barton," Stephen greeted him. "Long time, no see. What have you been up to?"

"Besides competing with you for the Perkins contract?" Matthias replied. "Not much."

Well, he'd recently lost his personal assistant of five years, Kendall thought irritably. Or so she'd heard. That was kind of major.

As if he'd read her mind, Matthias turned to her then and feigned tremendous surprise—though, Kendall thought, not very well.

"Why, Kendall Scarborough," he said with overblown amazement. "What are you doing here? I haven't seen you since…" He pretended to search his memory banks—again, not exactly an Academy Award-winning performance— then snapped his fingers. "Since you gave me your two weeks' notice to go work for some fly-by-night company."

She sighed wearily. "Well, except for this afternoon in my room, when you offered me my job back."

Now Stephen was the one to look surprised, Kendall noted. Only his was obviously genuine. Then he smiled, and looked at Matthias again. "Really?" he asked the other man.

Matthias looked a little uncomfortable now, and this time, he wasn't pretending. "It was just a formality," he said. "I always offer my exes the chance to come back, once they come to their senses and realize what a mistake they made, leaving Barton Limited."

Kendall couldn't prevent the snort of laughter that escaped her at that. Yeah, right. Matthias had the longest memory of anyone she'd ever met, and he never forgot a slight—real *or* imagined. If someone elected to leave the company for any reason, he had that person's personnel file expunged within the hour, as if they never existed. And he certainly never went looking for that person to offer them an opportunity to return.

Not until this afternoon, anyway, she reminded herself.

But the only reason he'd come looking for her, she further told herself, was because he hadn't known how to program his new BlackBerry. The offer to take her back had obviously been off-the-cuff, and had doubtless been extended for the same reason. He thought she was the only one who knew how to program one of those things. He didn't realize anyone could do it for him. Well, anyone except Matthias Barton.

"Well, Barton," Stephen said now, "had you appreciated Kendall's possibilities, the way I do, then maybe you wouldn't have lost her in the first place."

Kendall started to smile at that, then stopped. Something about the way Stephen had said it made it sound kind of unprofessional. Just what had he meant by *possibilities?* That was kind of a strange word to use. Why not *abilities?* Or *talents?* Or *expertise? Possibilities* made it sound as though he considered her a blank slate or unformed mass that he could turn into whatever he wanted.

"I assure you, DeGallo," Matthias replied, "that Kendall was one of my most prized possessions at Barton Limited. I hope you realize what an asset she'll be to OmniTech."

All right, Kendall thought. That did it. Forget about blank slates and unformed masses. Matthias had just made her sound like a new computer system. Possession? Asset? Just who did he think he was?

"Prized possession?" she echoed indignantly.

Matthias looked down at her and must have realized immediately from both her voice and her expression—and, most likely, the quick drop in temperature among the small group—what a colossal gaffe he'd just made. "Uh…" he began eloquently.

"If that's the case," she continued while he was still off balance, "then you better go over my operating instructions while you're here. I wouldn't want Stephen to think he acquired a defective machine."

The look Matthias gave her then was almost convincingly distressed. Almost. "Kendall, that's not—"

This time his words were cut off by Stephen's light, good-natured laughter. "Sounds to me like she works just fine," he said. "In fact, this particular model is promising to work better than I initially hoped."

Matthias's lips thinned at that. "Yeah, she's a piece of work, all right," he muttered.

She smiled sweetly. "And now I'm working for someone else."

Matthias opened his mouth to respond, but this time was prevented by the arrival of their server, who placed tall sweaty glasses of mineral water in front of Kendall and Stephen. Then the waiter looked at Matthias and asked, "Will you be joining this party?"

Even Matthias, Kendall thought, wouldn't be crass enough to crash her meeting with Stephen. And he didn't. Instead, he told their server that no, he was on his own and didn't want to interrupt anyone's dinner, so would just take a seat at a table by himself. Then, even though there were at least a dozen empty tables in the restaurant, he pulled out a chair from the table immediately beside Kendall's and Stephen's, and seated himself without a care.

Unbelievable, Kendall thought. Evidently, Matthias was that crass, after all. If not in blatantly joining them, then certainly in doing his best to destroy any chance the two of them might have for speaking freely about her new obligations as vice president. There was no way Stephen would discuss the policies of his company in the presence of one of his competitors, even superficially. He confirmed that by shrugging philosophically when Kendall looked at him—not that she needed any confirmation.

So instead of talking about her new job over the course of dinner, Kendall and Stephen instead discussed superficialities like the weather, books, current events and a favorite TV show they had in common…with Matthias throwing in his own commentaries here and there, completely uninvited.

It was going to be a long orientation.

Four

The temp Matthias ordered from a Tahoe City agency—once he found the phone book after thirty minutes of looking for it—arrived promptly at eight o'clock the morning after his arrival. Unfortunately, he'd done something wrong when he tried to set his alarm clock the night before—no, the alarm clock was defective, that was the problem—because it was the ringing of the front doorbell that alerted him to the arrival of his early-morning appointment. Not Kendall, who would have normally alerted Matthias to that. Kendall, too, would have been infinitely less intrusive about her reminder than the doorbell was.

Damn, he thought as he looked groggily at the clock and realized it had stopped working completely. He lifted his watch from the nightstand and grimaced when he saw the time. He never slept this late. And he'd never been unprepared for an appointment. Shoving off the covers, he jackknifed into a sitting position and scrubbed both hands briskly over his face to rouse himself. He grabbed a plain white T-shirt from the bag he hadn't even begun to unpack, shook it out quickly and thrust it over his head as he descended the stairs. And he thought dryly how lucky he was that it matched his sweatpants so well, otherwise he might have to be embarrassed about his attire. It was only as he was reaching for the doorknob that he realized he'd forgotten to put on shoes, so would be greeting his temporary employee barefoot. Somehow, though, he couldn't quite rouse the wherewithal to care.

The young man on the other side of the door looked surprised by Matthias's sudden appearance—and, doubtless, by his slovenly appearance—but quickly schooled his features into indifference. He obviously hadn't overslept, because he was well-groomed and dressed impeccably in a pale gray suit and white dress shirt, his necktie the only spot of color on his person—if you could consider pale yellow a color. He was young, early twenties at most, his blond hair cut short, his gray eyes nearly the same color as his suit. He looked to Matthias like something from a middle school poster advertising Junior Achievement.

"Mr. Barton?" he said.

Matthias ran a quick hand through his dark hair to tame it as best he could. "Yeah, that's me," he replied. Quickly, he amended, "I mean, yes. I'm Matthias Barton."

"William Denton," he said, extending his hand. "From DayTimers. I'm your new temp."

"Whoa, whoa, whoa," Matthias said, holding up a hand. "I haven't hired you yet."

This was clearly news to young William. "But they said

you need an assistant for the month you'll be spending here in Hunter's Landing," he said.

"I do need an assistant for the month," Matthias told him. "But I'm not going to take any Tom, Dick or William they send my way. I need to make sure you have all the qualifications I need for an assistant."

Young William smiled confidently. "No worries there, Mr. Barton. Temping is just my summer job. I earned my BS from the Haas School of Business at UC Berkeley in May, and I'll be returning in the fall to start work on my MBA. I'm more than qualified to take on this position."

Matthias's back went up at the kid's presumption. "Are you?" he asked coolly.

William Denton's confidence seemed to waver a bit. Nevertheless, he replied, "Yes. I am." As an afterthought, he added, "Sir."

Matthias nodded, settling his hands on his hips in challenge. They'd just see about that. Without even inviting William Denton into the lodge, he barked, "What are the major managerial and organizational challenges posed by electronic commerce?"

William Denton blinked as if a too-bright flash had gone off right in front of his eyes. "I…what?"

Matthias shook his head, sighed with much gusto, and asked, "All right, if that one's too tough, then how about this. True or false. In the simple Ricardian model, trade between similar economies is unlikely to generate large gains from that trade."

William Denton's lips parted in response to that one, but no words emerged to answer the question. Until, finally, he said, "I…what?"

Man, Matthias thought, this guy was never going to

amount to anything if he couldn't answer the most obvious question in the world. "All right, here's an easy one," he said. "Multiple choice. The current ratio and quick ratio are the best indicators of a company's what? A. liquidity, B. efficiency, C. profitability or D. growth rate."

William Denton's mouth began to work over that one—kind of—but his brain didn't seem to be cooperating.

Matthias shook his head in disappointment. "I'm sorry, Mr. Denton, but I just don't think you have what it takes to—"

"Wait!" he interrupted. "I know the answer to that one!"

"Unfortunately, your time is up," Matthias told him. "Tell DayTimers I'll be in touch."

And with that, he pushed the front door closed and turned away. From the other side, William Denton called out, "A! It's A! Liquidity! Right? Am I right?"

He was right, Matthias thought. But it was too little, too late. The person he hired as his assistant was going to have to be a quick thinker and unafraid to speak up, in addition to being knowledgeable and savvy. Like Kendall. William Denton just didn't have what it took to fill her shoes.

Oh, well. Another candidate lacking even the most rudimentary business skills. Another interview shot to hell. Matthias would just have to look for someone else.

Padding barefoot to the kitchen, he absently pushed the button on the coffeemaker, then went to retrieve the phone book from the same cabinet where he had discovered it the day before. Bypassing DayTimers this time—since, if William Denton was the best they could do, they were obviously a fly-by-night operation—he selected the next agency on the list. After arranging for a prospective temp to come to the lodge later in the day, Matthias turned to pour himself a cup of coffee—

Only to discover that the carafe on the hot pad was empty. In fact, the hot pad wasn't even hot. He was sure he'd filled the machine with both water and coffee the night before, but lifted the top, anyway, to make sure. Yep. Coffee on one side. Water on the other. Just like the directions said. He checked to make sure the machine was plugged in. Yep. It was. He made sure the cord was attached to the coffeemaker, as well, ensured that the light switch on the wall nearest the appliance was switched to the on position, in case that was necessary, inspected everything he could possibly inspect to see what the problem was. To no avail. He pushed the on button again. Nothing.

Dammit.

Matthias wasn't one of those pathetic caffeine addicts who couldn't function without their crack-of-dawn coffee and suffered ugly mood swings when denied. No way. But, like any civilized human being, he liked to enjoy a cup or two in the morning, maybe three if he had time, possibly four or five, if he had a meeting or something, and, okay maybe another jolt or two or three in the afternoon when he needed it. He didn't *have* to have coffee. He just wanted it. A lot.

He stared at the coffeemaker intently, drumming his fingers irregularly on the countertop, willing the machine to work. With great deliberation, he pushed the on button again. Nada.

Damn. His gaze lit then on a short stack of papers he'd placed on the countertop the night before. It was the last assignment Kendall had completed before she'd tendered her resignation, a contract she'd typed up for an agreement between Barton Limited and a new consulting firm with whom he'd be doing limited business for the rest of the year. He smiled, and reached for the phone again, punching in a number he knew by heart.

"Kendall," he said when she answered her cell phone. "It's…" He started to say "Mr. Barton," but halted. "Mathias," he identified himself instead. "There's a problem with the Donovan contract you typed up before you left. Can you spare a couple of hours this morning to go over it?" He listened to her objection, then said, "I realize that. But this is a problem you're responsible for, one you need to rectify. And it's urgent. When can you be here?" He grinned at her reply. "Good. I promise not to keep you any longer than I absolutely have to. And, Kendall," he added before she had a chance to hang up, "I saw a coffee shop in town. Would you mind swinging by it on your way?"

Kendall stewed as she waited for Matthias to answer the doorbell she'd just rung, and switched the enormous cardboard cup of coffee from one hand to the other as it began to burn her fingers. It had been awkward, to say the least, explaining to Stephen DeGallo on her first official day of training why she needed to take part of the morning off. And although he hadn't exactly been happy about the request, he'd told her to go ahead, that they could meet again after lunch.

Lunch, she thought now, that she should have been having with her new boss, not the one she'd left behind.

As if conjured by the thought, Matthias opened the door, smiling with what looked like profound relief when he saw her. She softened some at his expression, flattered that, in spite of everything, he still seemed to need her. It was always a nice feeling to have.

Then he reached for the massive cup of coffee in her hand, popped off the top and lifted it toward his face, inhaling deeply to enjoy a long, leisurely sniff. Carefully, he lifted it to his mouth and sipped, closing his eyes as he savored it. Then he opened them again, stared down into the dark brew and said, "Oh, God, that's better."

That was when Kendall realized it was the coffee for which he was grateful, not her. And she wondered again why she'd bothered.

Because she was conscientious about her work, she told herself. It had nothing to do with Matthias needing her. If there truly was a problem with the Donovan contract that was her fault, then it was, as he'd said, up to her to rectify it. Although she couldn't imagine what she'd done wrong. She'd triple- and quadruple-checked the document before she'd given it to Matthias to look at. And why was he just now looking at it, anyway? she wondered. It was supposed to have gone back to Elliot Donovan two weeks ago.

And what was up with his appearance? she wondered further. Okay, she knew he was on vacation, but she'd never seen him looking like this. Here it was, almost ten o'clock in the morning, and he looked as if he'd just rolled out of bed. His black sweatpants were rumpled from sleep, as was the white V-neck T-shirt stretched taut enough across his chest that she could see the dark hair beneath—besides what was visible around the neckline. A day's growth of beard shadowed his face, his dark hair was shaggy and uncombed and his brown eyes were hooded and soft. He looked…

Well, actually, Kendall thought as a coil of something warm and electric unwound in her belly, he looked kind of…hot.

No! Not hot! she immediately corrected herself. Slovenly. Yeah, that was it. Seeing him looking the way he did made her think of some lazy hedonist lolling in bed on a Sunday morning. Some dark-haired, sleepy-eyed pleasure monger, waking slowly and stretching his brawny arms high over his head, then smiling down at the woman lying next to him, who—Hey, how about that?—looked a lot like Kendall, then gliding a slow finger across my…I mean, *her*…naked shoulder, then leaning down to trace the same path with his mouth before rolling me…I mean, *her*…over onto her back and sliding his hand beneath the covers, down along my…I mean, *her*…naked torso and settling it between my…I mean, *her*…I mean…I mean…I mean…

She stifled a groan and stopped thinking about how Matthias looked. Until he lowered the cup of coffee again and ran his tongue along the seam of his lips to savor the lingering taste of it, wherein all Kendall could do was think about how it would feel to have his tongue running along the seam of her lips, too.

Oh. No.

The Donovan contract, she reminded herself. That was why she was here. Not for…anything else. "So, um…what's the, uh…the problem with the, ah…the Donovan contract," she finally got out.

For a moment, he looked at her as if he had no idea what she was talking about. Then, "Right," he finally said. "Come on in."

He stepped aside to let her enter, and as Kendall pushed past him, she tried not to notice how the fragrance of the coffee mingled with a scent that was distinctly Matthias, something spicy and woodsy whose source she'd never been able to identify. It was probably from the soap or shampoo that he used, though she'd never known another man to smell the way he did—or as good as he did. And smelling him again now, after being deprived for two weeks…

She sighed. What was the matter with her this morning? She was reacting to Matthias as if he were an old boyfriend she hadn't been ready to break up with.

She reminded herself again that she was nothing more to him than a former employee, and that he was nothing more to her than a former employer. She'd come here because of a professional obligation, not a personal one. The sooner she fixed whatever she'd done wrong with the Donovan contract, the sooner she could get back to work. Her new work. At her new job. With her new boss. One who appreciated her business degree and knowledge. One to whom she owed the greater obligation now. Matthias was her past. No, Barton Limited was her past, she corrected herself. And OmniTech Solutions was her future.

Period.

She spun around as Matthias closed the front door. "What's the problem?" she asked point blank.

Instead of answering her, he tilted his head toward the sweeping staircase behind him and said, "This way."

She rankled at the order, but followed him, noting how beautiful the lodge was. Wow. Whoever'd furnished the place had great taste. And they knew a thing or two about making a home comfortable without making it too feminine. Although the colors were bold and the fabrics a little masculine, Kendall would have felt perfectly content staying here herself. And the view of the lake beyond the picture windows was spectacular.

She wondered again about the details of the bequest that required him to be here. It must have been a pretty major requirement to make him take an entire month away from the office. Especially in a place like Lake Tahoe, where there were so few corporate concerns, and no one she could think of that Barton Limited did business with. Then again, in the whole time she'd worked for him, she couldn't remember him ever taking a vacation of more than a couple of days. So maybe it would do him good to be here for a month. Maybe he'd learn to relax a little. Realize there was more to life than work.

Yeah, right, she thought. And maybe the next World Wrestling champion would be named Stone Cold Sheldon Abernathy.

As her foot hit the stairway landing, her gaze lit on a photograph that was hanging there, and Matthias's reasons for being in the lodge became clearer. Unable to stop herself, Kendall halted for a moment, smiling at the picture of the—she quickly counted—seven men, all college-aged, one of whom was obviously Matthias. But one was his twin brother, Luke, too, so she wasn't sure, at first, which was which. Then she noted the way one of the boys' smiles curled up a little more on one side than the other, and she knew, without question, it was Matthias. Interestingly, he was the one with the longer hair, and was the more raggedly dressed of the two. Funny, because Matthias had always talked about his brother as if Luke were the black sheep of the family, the rebel, the one who wanted to make waves. Looking at the photograph, however, it was Matthias who better fit that description.

"The contract is in the office," she heard him say from some distance away.

Looking up, she saw that he had continued to the second floor and was striding down the hall without realizing she had stopped. "Hey!" she called after him, surprising herself. She'd never said *Hey!* to Matthias before. It had always been *Excuse me, sir* or *Pardon me, Mr. Barton,* something that had been in keeping with their relationship—which had always been fairly formal. It was just that, being here in this beautiful, comfortable lodge with him, seeing him in sweats and a T-shirt and finding a picture of him from his youth, formal was the last thing she felt.

He spun around at the summons, at first looking as surprised by the casual address as she'd been. Then he saw what she was looking at and...

Huh, she thought. She would have thought he would smile in much the same way as he was smiling in the photograph. Instead, he looked kind of annoyed. Probably because he didn't want an employee—even a former one—seeing him as anything but the businessman that he was.

Well, tough, she retorted silently. If that was the case, he shouldn't have made her drive down here. And he certainly shouldn't have answered the door in his jammies.

He walked slowly back down the hall, and then the stairs, until he stood beside her, hooking his hands on his hips in a way that made him look very put out. "What?" he asked. Interestingly, he didn't look at the picture, even though he had to realize that was why she'd called him back.

Unfortunately, she suddenly realized she wasn't sure what she'd intended to say when she'd called him back. She'd mostly just wanted to look at him now and compare him to the boy in the photograph. So she pointed to the picture and said, "Who are these guys you're with?"

It was with obvious reluctance that Matthias turned to look at the picture. He studied it for only a moment, then turned back to Kendall. "Friends from college. We called ourselves the Seven Samurai."

"Akira Kurosawa fans, were you?" she asked, proud of herself for knowing the name of the director of the film made half a century ago.

"Actually, I think Hunter was the only one of us who even saw the movie. He's the one who named us. God knows why."

"Which one is Hunter?" Kendall asked.

With even more reluctance than before, Matthias lifted his hand and pointed at the young man who was laughing right at the camera. He looked the happiest of the bunch, and gave the impression, even on film, of being their ringleader.

"Where is he now?" Kendall asked.

Matthias hesitated a telling moment before revealing, "He died."

Something hard and cold twisted in Kendall's belly at hearing the flatness of Matthias's voice. Even more than he sounded sad, he sounded…tired. As if the weight of his friend's death was too much for him to bear.

"What happened?" she asked softly. "He was so young."

"Melanoma," he said. "This is his lodge, even though he never lived to see it completed."

"I'm so sorry, Matthias," she said quietly. Impulsively, she extended a hand and curled her fingers over his upper arm, giving it a gentle, reassuring squeeze. His skin was warm beneath her fingers, solid, strong. But in that moment, he didn't seem any of those things himself. "I didn't mean to bring up bad memories," she told him.

He shook his head. "Actually, since coming here, I've had one or two good memories," he told her. "Things I'd forgotten about." He did smile then, albeit sadly. Still, it was better to see that than the look of desolation that had clouded his features a moment ago.

She waited to see if he would elaborate on his memories, but he didn't. And Kendall didn't want to pry any further than she already had. Even if she was massively curious about the other young men in the picture. And even more curious about the young Matthias.

"So the rest of you will share the house now?" she asked.

"None of us owns the place," he told her. "But each of us is spending a month here before it goes to its rightful owner. Which will be the town of Hunter's Landing."

Kendall smiled. She hadn't made the connection until now. "So Hunter came from here? Or he's named after the place?"

Matthias shook his head. "No, I think he just stumbled onto the town and liked that it shared his name. And since it was on the lake, he thought it was the perfect spot for the lodge. We'd all talked about doing something like this in college, building a big party house we'd share someday, but after graduation, we never followed through. We were all too *busy*," he said, the last word sounding as if it left a bad taste in his mouth. "Busy *working*," he added, emphasizing that word in a way that was even less complimentary. Which was strange, since Matthias was the kind of man for whom busyness was one of the seven virtues and for whom work was sheer Nirvana. "Too busy working for useless things like following dreams," he concluded softly.

His expression had gone soft, too, as he spoke, Kendall noticed, and when he turned away from the picture to look at her again, there was something in his eyes she'd never seen before. Melancholy. It was almost tangible.

"So do you still see the other Samurai?" she asked. "Besides your brother, I mean?"

Who, she had to admit, he hadn't seen much of. It had only been a couple of months ago that the brothers had even spoken to each other after years of estrangement. And then only because Matthias had needed Luke to switch months at the cabin with him so he could take his trip to Stuttgart. It had been that or break the terms of the will, and Matthias hadn't wanted to do that. Neither had Luke, which was the only reason he'd gone along with the switch. Ultimately, once everything with Lauren Conover had been smoothed out, the Barton brothers had renewed their relationship. But it was still, Kendall knew, a little strained at times.

Matthias looked at the picture again, seeming to take in each of the men one by one. "I haven't seen any of them for years," he said. "Though we'll all be here for the dedication in September."

"What dedication?" Kendall echoed.

He nodded, still looking at the photograph. "Once each of us has spent a month here, the house will go to the town, and I think the plan is to turn it into some kind of medical facility or something. Anyway, there's going to be a big ceremony with the mayor and chamber of commerce or something. All of us will be here, too."

She smiled. "Sounds like Hunter was a good guy."

"The best," Matthias immediately replied. " He was the very best of all of us." This time, when he smiled, there was genuine warmth, and genuine happiness, in the gesture. Then the smile fell, and he grimaced a bit. "I'm sorry. I'm keeping you longer than I meant to."

Actually, Kendall thought, *she* was the one who was holding up things by asking all these questions. *She* was the one who would make herself even later than she'd intended getting back to Stephen DeGallo. Funny, though, how she hadn't given Stephen a thought since entering the lodge.

"Hey," she said again when he started to turn away, more softly than she had the first time.

He spun around again. "What?"

She smiled and pointed to him in the photo. "You looked good with long hair."

He looked at where she was pointing and asked, "Are you so sure that one's me? It could be Luke."

She shook her head. "No, I know it's you."

Now he crossed his arms over his chest, as if in challenge. "How do you know?"

She wasn't about to tell him she knew him by his roguish smile. So she said, "I can tell by the twinkle in your eyes."

Oh, bravo, Kendall, she congratulated herself. *Telling him that was so much better than telling him you recognized him by his smile.*

Matthias arched his eyebrows at the comment, his eyes... Oh, damn. They were twinkling. "Really?" he asked with much interest. Way more interest than he should be showing, actually.

"I mean..." Kendall started to backtrack.

But he wasn't going to let her. "You think my eyes twinkle? Since when?"

"Well, since you were in college, anyway," she hedged. She pointed at the photograph again. "Obviously."

"No, I mean, since when did *you* notice it?" he asked.

If she were going to be honest, she would have to admit that she first noticed it when he interviewed her for the job. Naturally, she wouldn't tell him that. "I don't know," she hedged again. "And really, it's not like they twinkle a lot or anything."

He smiled. "They must, if that's how you knew it was me in the photo and not Luke."

"Okay, I lied," she said. "That's not how I knew it was you in the picture."

His smile grew broader. He was enjoying this, she thought. Enjoying seeing her uncomfortable. Enjoying putting her on the spot. She eyed him carefully. Or was it that he was enjoying the fact that she'd noticed his eyes? she wondered.

Nah, she assured herself. He couldn't have cared less what she noticed about him. He was just having fun at her expense.

"Then if it wasn't my twinkling eyes," he said, "what was it?"

She sighed with exasperation. At herself, because if she'd been put on the spot, it wasn't Matthias who'd put her there. She'd gone willingly by opening her mouth in the first place. Oh, hell, she thought. She'd already blown it. So she answered honestly this time, "It's your smile, okay? I could tell it was you because of your smile."

A smile that bloomed full force when he heard that. Honestly, Kendall thought. There should be a vaccination for the way Matthias could make a woman feel by turning on the full wattage of his smile.

"Really?" he asked. "What's so special about it?"

"Oh, you're just fishing now," she told him.

"Damned right. It's not every day a beautiful woman compliments a man's smile."

It was for him, Kendall thought. She was sure of—

Then the rest of what he said hit her. "You think I'm beautiful?"

His smile faltered at that. "Did I say that?"

She nodded. Vigorously. "Yes. You did."

He shifted his weight from one foot to the other, clearly not feeling as confident as he'd been a second ago. "Are you sure?"

"Yes. I am." What, did he think she didn't notice it when a man said she was beautiful? Especially a man like him?

"Well, I…" he began. "I mean…" he continued. "It's just…" he hedged this time.

"What?" Kendall demanded.

He jutted his thumb over his shoulder and said, "The Donovan contract. We really need to take a look at that."

She opened her mouth to object, but Matthias had already spun around on his heel and was headed down the hall. Knowing it would be pointless to continue—for now—Kendall followed him.

She found herself in an office decorated as nicely as the rest of the house, all warm wood paneling and hardwood floors and bold colors and boxy, but comfortable, furniture. There was a desk on which sat Matthias's laptop—she'd recognize it anywhere, even without the San Francisco Giants wallpaper—a chair, some shelves and a massive bulletin board onto which someone had tacked and taped more old photos of Matthias and his other six Samurai.

Then her gaze lit on a handwritten note that was tacked up alongside them. "Matt," it began—Matt? Kendall thought.

Good luck, bud. You're about to begin your month at "the Love Shack." Remember the universal truths about women we came up with on New Year's Eve our senior year? Scrap 'em. Here are the new universal truths about The One: She'll set you free. Loving her is the most dangerous thing you'll ever do.

It was signed, "Ryan."

Matt? Kendall thought again. She couldn't imagine anyone calling Matthias *Matt.* Then she remembered the way he'd looked in the photograph and altered her opinion. She supposed, once upon a time, he could have been a *Matt* after all. But what was with this "love shack" business?

"Here it is," Matthias said, picking up the document in question and dispelling any further ruminations she might have had on the love shack thing. "There are actually three places where I found errors," he added as he flipped up the top page.

Three? Kendall wondered. How could there have been that many? She'd gone over it a million times.

"The first one is on page two," he said.

She moved to stand beside him, so she could see what he was talking about, and tried again to ignore the luscious fragrance that was coffee and Matthias Barton.

He pointed to the middle of the second paragraph and said, "You left out a comma here."

Certain she'd misunderstood, she looked up at him and said, "What?"

He pointed again. "A comma," he repeated. "You left one out here. This is a compound sentence. There should be a comma before *and* here. And then on page three," he said, quickly turning the next page, "in the first paragraph here, this semicolon should be a comma, too. I'm sure of it. And on the last page," he continued, flipping back to that, "you didn't make the signature line long enough.

There should be at least another quarter inch there, to allow space for Donovan to sign. His first name is Elliot. You don't want to add insult to injury, not giving the man enough room to sign his name."

Kendall couldn't believe her ears. *This* was the problem with the Donovan contract? A comma? A semicolon? A signature line? For *this,* she'd risked hacking off her new boss? For *this* she'd driven a half hour one way? For *this* she'd bought him coffee using money out of her own pocket?

But even more offensive than all that was the fact that he was completely wrong. There was absolutely no need for a comma where he said there was—that wasn't a compound sentence—and the semicolon was perfectly fine. As for the sig line, she'd seen Elliot Donovan's signature before, and a more cramped bit of writing didn't exist anywhere. There was more than enough room for the man to sign his name.

She narrowed her eyes at Matthias. "You brought me all the way down here for a comma, a semicolon and a signature line?"

He clearly didn't see anything wrong with that. "It's details like that, Kendall, that people notice."

"Not unless they're wrong. Which these aren't," she told him.

He looked surprised at that. "Really?"

"Really."

"You're sure?"

"I'm sure."

"Oh. Well. Then I guess I brought you down here for nothing."

If looks could kill, Kendall thought, Matthias would be radioactive wind just then.

"But now that you're here," he said, "why don't you stay for lunch? The caretaker left some great stuff in the fridge."

There were so many ways Kendall could have answered his question—not the least of which was head-butting him, something she very much wanted to do just then—so she settled on a simple, "No. Thank you," and hoped he would hear the edge in her voice. And then, you know, fear for his life.

Instead, he smiled and asked, "Then how about if I offer you your old job back, and then you won't have to worry about getting back to Stephen DeGallo on time, because you'll already be where you need to be."

At that, Kendall decided that head-butting was too good for Matthias. What he really deserved was being hit with a brick. No, two bricks. Oh, what the hell. The same number of bricks it took to build the British Museum. However, she again managed to reply, "No. Thank you." And then she added, "Now, if you'll excuse me, I have to, as you said, go where I need to be. Which is *not* here."

And with that, she spun on her heel and exited the office. Without looking back once. Without even saying goodbye.

Five

Matthias watched Kendall through the front window of the cabin as she descended the steps toward her car.

He'd told her the truth about having good memories of Hunter and the rest of the gang since coming to the lodge. But he'd been plagued by even more bad ones. Not just of Hunter's death, but of how he and Luke had let their own relationship fall apart. Hunter had been the one in college who'd somehow managed to help the brothers turn their competition with each other into affection for each other. When he died, it was almost as if the bond that had held Matthias and Luke together died, too.

Matt and Luke, he corrected himself. Back then, he hadn't been Matthias. He'd been Matt. A regular guy, an easygoing student, the kind of kid who liked keggers and Three Stooges movies and games of pickup rugby in the park. It had only been after college, when he'd heard the terms of his father's will, that he'd begun to go by his given name of Matthias. Matthias had sounded more studied than Matt, more serious, more seasoned. Matthias had sounded like a grown-up. And, thanks to the terms of his father's will, Matt had been forced to grow up fast.

Even in death, the old man had pitted the twin brothers against each other, decreeing that whoever was able to make the first million would win the estate in its entirety. The one who didn't would be left with nothing. When the attorneys had read the stipulation to him and Luke, Matthias had been able to picture their father in the afterlife, leaning back in his celestial Barcalounger, rubbing his hands together with relish and saying, "Let the games begin."

And at first it had kind of been a game. Luke and Matthias had each good-naturedly joked that they would leave the other in the dust. Both had started their own companies, and then got down to business. Literally. For the first couple of months, they'd gone at it as they had every other competition they'd indulged in over the years, be it for a game, or a grade, or a girl. Then, little by little, Matthias had started edging ahead. A deal here, an acquisition there, and the money had begun to pile higher. A hundred thousand. Two hundred and fifty thousand. Half a million. Until that final deal that had cinched it for him and ensured he would win.

The problem was that the final deal had been tainted—unbeknownst to Matthias at the time—by some shady dealings inside his own company. Luke, suspicious, had cried foul and accused Matthias of cheating, an accusation Matthias resoundingly denied for years. An accusation that had split the brothers to the point of not speaking. Until Matthias discovered—only recently, in fact—a rat in his own corporation who had double-dealed him and Luke both and then disappeared with his own ill-gotten gains. And even though the two brothers realized now that they'd both been taken advantage of back then—even though the lines of communication were open now—things still weren't quite settled. Yeah, Matthias had helped his brother win the woman he'd once planned to marry himself. That the help had come in the form of a punch to Luke's eye had just been cake. But Luke had apologized for being an ass. Matthias, in turn, had apologized for being an ass *and* not trying harder to keep the lines of communication open.

Those lines were open now, he reminded himself. But things with Luke still weren't where they should be. He supposed there would never again be a day when they were the carefree college kids Hunter had helped them to be. But they could be brothers again.

And they would, he vowed. He would start calling his brother on a regular basis and make sure they saw more of each other. Hell, they both lived in San Francisco. It wasn't as if it was a hardship for them to see each other.

Kendall had folded herself into her car by now and started the ignition, and was looking over her shoulder as she backed out of the drive. She stopped to wait for a dog to trot past before pulling out, and when she did, for some reason, she looked back up at the house. Her eyes immediately connected with his, but she'd donned sunglasses, so it was impossible to read her expression. Matthias lifted a hand to wave it in halfhearted farewell and, after a moment, she lifted a hand in response. But she didn't wave, and she didn't smile, so the gesture felt more final than it should have.

And then she was rolling out of the driveway and putting

the car in gear, and heading down the road that would take her back to the highway. She didn't turn around again, even when she braked for the stop sign. Matthias watched her car until she was out of sight, then stood at the window a little longer, watching the empty place in the road where last he'd seen her. He told himself to get busy, that he had a lot of work to do today. He reminded himself he had another temp coming by in a few hours.

He reminded himself of a lot of things as he stood at the window looking at the place where Kendall wasn't. But all he could remember was the way her hand had felt, curled tentatively over his arm when she'd expressed her sympathy over Hunter's death.

She was going where she thought she needed to be, he told himself, recalling the words he'd used first, and which she'd turned back on him in an entirely different—and erroneous—way. But she was wrong. She didn't *need to be* with Stephen DeGallo, a man who would only use her long enough to pick her brain about Matthias's business and then manufacture some excuse to let her go. The man didn't like people working closely with him whom he hadn't brought up himself from scratch. Matthias knew DeGallo fairly well—What was the old adage? Keep your friends close, your enemies closer?—and Kendall, to DeGallo's way of thinking, was tainted. She was used goods, sloppy seconds. No matter how much she liked and trusted the guy, DeGallo would, once he got the information from her he wanted, consider her a liability, and he would let her go.

And *that,* Matthias told himself as he continued to watch the empty street, was why he needed—no, *wanted*—Kendall to come back to work for Barton Limited. Because

DeGallo didn't appreciate her the way Matthias did. Because DeGallo wouldn't offer her the security and benefits Matthias would. Because DeGallo didn't care about her any more than he would care about a new printer or phone system or hard drive.

It *wasn't* because of the warmth that had spread through him when she'd curled her fingers around his arm. And it wasn't because of the way she'd looked at him as he'd talked about his old friends, as if she wanted to hear more—about them *and* him. And it certainly wasn't because the lodge had come alive while she was here and felt dim and somber now that she was gone. That was ridiculous. Houses didn't live and they didn't have feelings.

Then again, there were those who would say the same thing about Matthias.

He sighed heavily and pushed a handful of hair back from his forehead. He didn't have time for this, he thought. He had work to do and an interview to perform. Because as much as he knew Kendall wasn't where she needed to be, she was the one who would have to realize that. In the meantime, he needed—no, wanted—someone else.

Even if no one else would ever come close to her.

By the end of the week, Matthias had run through every temp agency in the Tahoe area without finding even a marginally acceptable candidate to replace Kendall, even temporarily. The one who had just appeared at his door was his very last hope, and already he knew she wasn't going to work out, either. She had no concept of how to dress for a job interview, even one conducted in a nonoffice environment. She'd actually paired a crisp white shirt with a pair of pin-striped trousers and flat loafers, and had knotted her dark hair on the top of her head like a tennis ball. Her little black glasses were tailored and elegant, and her makeup—if she was even wearing any—was understated and clean.

What the hell was she thinking, showing up for a job interview looking like this? She was even more over-the-top and under-a-rock than the first guy had been.

He expelled a restless sigh and gestured halfheartedly toward the living room, indicating she should take a seat on one of the chairs beside the fireplace while he folded himself perfunctorily into the other. The sooner they got this interview over with, the better. Then Matthias could...

Well, okay, he could be alone. At least he wouldn't be wasting his time interviewing people who obviously had no clue how to interact in the world of big business. Instead, he'd be wasting his time dreading the fact that he'd have to set up another interview with someone who would almost certainly be as unqualified to fill Kendall's position as this woman was.

"So, Ms...." He glanced down at the résumé the temp agency had e-mailed him to inspect in preparation for her arrival. "Ms. Carrigan," he finished. "I see you're a graduate of Stanford Business School."

She smiled a small, unobtrusive smile that made Matthias flinch, so blatantly inappropriate was it for a job interview. "I am," she said. "I graduated in May with honors."

Yeah, yeah, yeah, Matthias thought. Honors schmonors. If he had a dollar for every honors degree places like Stanford and Harvard issued, he could paper the whole top of his desk.

"And what interests you about the position as my personal assistant?"

She sat up straighter, crossed her legs at the ankles,

wove her fingers together loosely in her lap, then tilted her head thoughtfully to one side. Matthias mentally shook his own head and somehow refrained from rolling his eyes. Her entire posture just screamed indolent slob. What an incredible waste of time this was.

"May I speak frankly, Mr. Barton?" she asked.

"Of course," he told her. Adding to himself, *Making presumptions already?*

"Ultimately," she began, "I'd like to move higher on the corporate ladder, but I think this would be a good entry level position for me, because it would offer me the opportunity to learn from, well, if you'll forgive my momentary gushing, a legend in the business world."

Suck-up, Matthias thought. But he kept his expression bland.

"University courses," she continued, "can only go so far in imparting information. I'm hoping that by coming to work for you fresh out of college, Mr. Barton, I could gain some professional experience that would enhance what I learned in the classroom at Stanford. At the same time, I'll do an excellent job keeping your schedule organized and making sure you have everything you need at any given moment. All modesty aside, my organizational skills are exemplary, and as you can see from the letters of recommendation I've supplied from five of my professors, I routinely led my classes when it came to completing assignments promptly and neatly."

Bighead, Matthias thought. Megalomaniac was more like it. Not to mention she was barely articulate enough to string two words together.

"I see," he said. "Well, that's all good information to have, and I appreciate your coming in today." He stood and extended his hand to her. "I have your résumé. I'll be in touch."

She was obviously surprised by the quickness with which he'd concluded the interview, but there was no reason for Matthias to waste any more time—hers or his. The woman had absolutely nothing to recommend her and was in no way suitable.

What was up with business schools these days? Matthias wondered as he watched her leave. Between Tahoe and San Francisco, he'd interviewed more than two dozen people to fill Kendall's position, and each person had been worse than the one before.

Well, there was nothing else for him to do, he thought. He couldn't afford to wait for Kendall to come to her senses. He'd just have to do or say whatever it took to get her back. Give her another raise, better benefits, whatever it took. Never mind that he'd already tried to do that. Twice. Never mind that he'd failed. Twice. Matthias Barton hadn't risen to the level of success he had by taking no for an answer. Unless, you know, no was the answer he wanted to hear. No *wasn't* a word he'd heard often from Kendall. Until, you know, recently. He was sure if he made her the right offer, she'd come around. Everyone had their price. Even Kendall. All Matthias had to do was find it.

Fortunately for him, he knew exactly where to look.

Kendall had been waiting for Stephen in the dining room of the Timber Lake Inn for fifteen minutes when she looked up at the restaurant's entrance once more, hoping to see her new employer there, and instead saw Matthias. He was dressed casually again, this time pairing his khaki trousers with a chocolate-brown polo that lovingly molded his broad chest and shoulders. She was surprised to see that he'd left his shirttail out, a casual affectation he normally didn't adopt. Then again, there was something about him tonight that suggested it wasn't an affectation at all.

She waited for the irritation that should have come at seeing him, but instead, she was filled with a strange sort of relief. Her orientation this week hadn't been quite what she'd thought it would be, filled as it had been with mostly one-on-one meetings with Stephen. Meetings that had taken place more often in restaurants than in a conference room at the hotel—conference rooms that were better suited to serving high tea than conducting business, anyway. Worse, the meetings had seemed to veer off course on a fairly regular basis, shifting from the policies and procedures of OmniTech to Kendall's experiences working with Matthias.

She didn't want to believe Matthias was right about Stephen DeGallo's only hiring her to uncover information about him. But after the way the week had gone, with her having to sidestep every effort Stephen made to shift the conversation to Barton Limited, Kendall couldn't quite dissuade herself of the idea that Matthias knew what he was talking about. At best, her new employer's training methods were unconventional. At worst, her new employer's intentions were underhanded. Either way, Kendall wasn't sure she was working for the right man. Either way, she wasn't sure she was where she needed to be.

Matthias caught her eye just as she completed that last thought, and a thrill of something hot and electric shuddered through her. She recognized it as sexual, but was surprised by its strength. Surprising, too, was how much it differed from the sexual responses she'd had to men in the past. Because joining the physical sensations that were rocketing through her body was an emotional reaction that was blooming in her heart. She had feelings for Matthias she hadn't had for other men. And they were stronger, she realized now, than she'd allowed herself to believe.

But this was *Matthias,* she tried to remind herself. As recently as a few weeks ago, he'd been Mr. Barton. Yes, she'd known she was attracted to him. But she'd thought removing herself from him would put an end to that attraction. Remove the appetite by removing the temptation. But the only thing removing the temptation had done was make her hungrier.

As long as she'd been working for him, Kendall's ethics hadn't allowed her to cross the line into intimacy. Office romances, she knew, were a Very Bad Idea, no matter how you played them. So as long as she was working for Barton Limited, her conscience had allowed her to find her boss attractive, but hadn't permitted her to act on that attraction. By leaving the office environment, any obstacles that had stood in the way of her feelings for him had disappeared. Simply put, now that she wasn't his employee anymore, her conscience and her brain—not to mention her heart—were letting in things they had locked up tight before.

Not good, she thought as he came to a stop behind the chair across from her and curled his fingers over the back of it. Because how wise would it be to let herself start feeling things—things beyond attraction—for a married man? Especially when what the man was married to was his business?

"Hi," he said. And with that one word, her troubled thoughts completely evaporated.

There would be plenty of time for thinking later, she told

herself. Especially if Stephen DeGallo never showed up. Where was he, anyway? It wasn't like him to be late. Then again, why did she care when Matthias was here?

That thought, more than any of the others she'd had this evening—this week—told her more than anything else could about herself. And her feelings. And her wisdom. Or lack thereof. What told her even more was how she quickly smoothed a hand over her ivory shirt and brown trousers before running it back over her head to make sure her hair was in place. Somehow, she knew she wouldn't have bothered for Stephen. Nor would she have removed her glasses to get a better look at him, as she did with Matthias now.

"Hi," she replied, tucking her glasses into her shirt pocket.

"Meeting DeGallo?" he asked.

She hesitated before telling him she feared her new boss had stood her up. Because then Matthias would ask her why, and she'd have to tell him she didn't know, unless maybe it was because Stephen had decided she wasn't a team player, even without first letting her into the dugout. So she only said, "Actually, I'm here alone." Which was true. She was alone. She just wasn't *supposed* to be alone.

And boy, was that a loaded statement she would just as soon not leave hanging. So she hurried on, "What are you doing here? Again?"

She hadn't meant for that *again* to sound as pointed as it had. Matthias either didn't notice or chose to pretend he hadn't heard it himself, because he only smiled and replied, "I actually came here to see if you wanted to have dinner with me. When you didn't answer my knock at you door upstairs, I took a chance that you'd be down here."

She nodded sagely, but said nothing.

He looked at her expectantly, but said nothing.

It occurred to her that he was waiting for her to invite him to sit down. Then it occurred to her that, with her luck, the minute she did, Stephen DeGallo would walk through the door with a perfectly legitimate reason for being so late, and whisk her off to a PowerPoint presentation of some of OmniTech's most arcane secrets, then apologize for it taking so long to invite her into the loving bosom of his inner sanctum.

And she thought, Ew. That sounded really gross.

Not to mention it was almost certainly *not* going to happen. At least, not that last part. But there was still a possibility that Stephen would show up with a legitimate reason for being late, and it wouldn't look good for her to be sitting here with Matthias.

"If you're waiting for Stephen," he began, as if he were able to read her thoughts.

"I'm not," she quickly interjected.

"Good," he said. "Because I saw him driving off with a breathtaking blonde as I was coming into the inn."

She gaped at him. "You did not. We had a dinner…" She started to say "date," realized that hammered home even better—or, rather, worse—what her orientation this week had felt like, and immediately corrected herself by finishing, "Appointment."

"So you *were* expecting him," Matthias said, a note of unmistakable triumph in his voice.

She flattened her mouth into a thin line to keep herself from saying anything else.

"Looks like your new boss stood you up, Kendall," Matthias said. "Which isn't a very sound business plan on his part." He hesitated a beat before adding, "The man's an idiot if he doesn't realize how lucky he is to have hired you."

The momentary thrill of surprise and pleasure that came with Matthias's compliment was quickly replaced by other things she felt for Stephen DeGallo. Resentment, frustration, disappointment. She was sure the two of them were supposed to have met for dinner here tonight. Positive. In fact, he'd told her barely three hours ago that he'd see her at six-thirty in the dining room.

She looked at her watch. It was ten till seven now. There was little chance the man would be this late when he was staying at the same hotel. Obviously, he'd discovered something—or someone—in the last few hours who had seemed a more profitable return on his investment.

She braced herself for Matthias's *I told you so,* but all he said was, "How about I buy you dinner instead?"

She told herself to say no, that all she really wanted to do was go up to her suite for some room service and a long bubble bath. Then she realized that was the last thing she wanted to do. She was tired of going to her room alone at night. Tired of wondering what Stephen's motives were in hiring her. Tired of not knowing if she'd made the right choice in coming to work for him.

Work, hah, she thought. Nothing she had experienced with Stephen DeGallo so far had felt anything like work. It had felt like…

Bribery, she thought. And snooping. And something kind of smarmy and icky.

She sighed again, but this time there was less resentment, frustration and disappointment in it. They were replaced instead with a sad sort of resolution that she had made a mistake. Not in leaving Matthias's employ, but in taking the job with OmniTech. She'd talk to Stephen tomorrow, ask him point-blank if he'd offered her the job because he'd expected her to tell him about the workings of Barton Limited. If he had, she would tender her resignation immediately. And if he hadn't...

Well. She'd wait to make plans until the two of them had had a chance to talk. In the meantime, she had another choice to make. And she told herself she'd better make the right one this time.

But instead of responding to Matthias's dinner invitation the way her brain told her to—by declining—she listened to her heart instead. Even knowing her heart was wont to get her into trouble. Hey, it wasn't as though her head had been doing such a good job lately.

"Dinner would be nice," she told him.

He smiled, and the heat inside Kendall sparked a little hotter. "Not here, though," he told her. "The steak I had the other night left a lot to be desired."

That wasn't the only thing at the Timber Lake Inn that was like that, Kendall thought.

"But I do know just the place. It's a bit of a drive, but you'll love it. Nice ambience, and the food is excellent. And the service can't be beat."

Before giving her a chance to agree or decline, he moved behind her chair and gave it a gentle tug. Then he lowered a hand to help her out of it. Without thinking about what she was doing, Kendall curled her fingers over his, marveling at how the heat inside her began to purl through her entire body.

This wasn't good, she told herself again as she rose. She should have told Matthias she couldn't go to dinner with him. It would be a mistake to think anything that might happen between them would ever go anywhere. Even if the two of them did get involved—and oh, wasn't she presuming a lot there?—whatever happened would flare up and fizzle out, probably in a very short time. Matthias Barton wasn't a man for relationships. He wasn't even a man for affection. The only thing he would ever love to distraction was his business.

As long as Kendall reminded herself of that—over and over and over again, she told herself—she would be fine. Right?

Of course, right.

Six

"You'll change your mind about this place, Kendall, the minute you taste your first glass of wine."

Matthias realized his concerns were unfounded when he turned from unlocking the lodge's front door to see Kendall gazing back at him with a smile. "That's okay," she said. "I like this place. It's nice. It makes you feel comfortable as soon as you enter."

So she'd noticed it, too, he thought. Interesting.

"Not to mention it's Friday night," he added. "Every decent place along the lake is going to be packed by now. We wouldn't get seated until after ten."

"It's nice that you have this place for a month," she said as she circled around him into the foyer. "It'll do you good."

It had already done him good, Matthias thought. And just by inviting Kendall inside, the good had become better.

"Remind me after it gets dark to go out onto the deck,"

he said as he closed the door behind them. "There's a telescope out there. It's incredible, the things you can find in the sky out here."

She smiled. "You've been looking through a telescope at night?"

He eyed her warily. "You sound surprised."

"I *am* surprised," she told him. "Matthias, you've never taken time out of your days—or nights—for something like that."

"Sure I have. I do it all the time."

She shook her head. "No, you don't."

"Yeah," he countered, a little more defensively than he would have liked. "I do."

Still smiling, she crossed her arms over her midsection. Inevitably, he noticed how, when she did that, the outline of her bra was just discernible enough through the pale fabric of her shirt to allow him to see that it was lace. He never would have pegged Kendall as the lacy lingerie type. She seemed like the Hanes-all-over type. Hell, there'd been times when she was working for him that she seemed like the boxer short type. And during one particularly daunting week, the jockstrap type. But now that he realized she *was* the lacy lingerie type…

Hmm. Actually, he found the idea kind of arousing. He also found himself wondering if she was the type to match bra to panties. Or, better yet, bra to thong bikini.

"Name one frivolous thing you do in your spare time," she challenged.

Figuring Kendall meant *besides* pondering the mysteries of her underwear, he opened his mouth to rattle off a dozen things he did for enjoyment, then realized he couldn't think of even one. Other than looking through the telescope, which he'd done only since coming here.

Finally, "I play squash," he said. "And tennis. And I play an occasional round of golf."

"And you use them all for networking and wheeling and dealing."

Yeah, okay, she had a point. So sue him.

He bristled at her suggestion that he was a man who found no enjoyment in life outside his work. Mostly because he couldn't honestly deny it. "Frivolity is overrated," he finally said. "And there's no point to it. I like working. It gives me pleasure. I don't need anything else in my life."

Her smile fell at that, and he realized he had been speaking with more vehemence than he intended—not to mention more than he felt. She'd just hit a sore spot with him, that was all. Why did everyone criticize people who were enthusiastic about their work? So what if he defined himself by how successful he was, and how hard he worked? So what if he was the kind of person who *would* be lying on his deathbed worrying that he hadn't worked enough during his life. There was nothing else in his life but work. Why was that such a terrible thing?

Kendall dropped her hands to her sides, her smile gone now. An awkward moment followed where neither seemed to know what to say. So Matthias forced himself to relax and said, "So how about dinner?"

For a minute, he thought—feared—she was going to decline and ask him to take her back to the inn. Finally, however, she nodded.

He roused a smile for her, tilting his head toward the kitchen. "Come on," he said in a lighter voice. "I'll have it on the table in ten minutes."

It actually only took about half that time, since all

Matthias had to do was remove food from containers in the fridge and arrange them on two plates. Opening the wine was the most time-consuming part of the task, but the cork left the bottle of Shiraz with a nice crisp *pop*. He poured them each a glass and carried those, too, to the table.

Kendall surveyed the food on the plate—a strip steak, green beans and new potatoes he'd picked up at a gourmet carryout place about ten miles down the road—a little warily.

"It's cold," she said.

"No, it's tartare," he countered as he sat in the chair on the side of the table that was perpendicular to hers. To show her it was fine, he lifted his fork and knife and sliced through the tender beef, then halved a potato with the side of his fork. "See? Looks delicious, doesn't it?"

"Tartare means uncooked," Kendall corrected him. She pointed at the plate. "This has been cooked. It just hasn't been heated up. I mean, even the vegetables are cold. Why don't you just pop the plates into the microwave for a couple of minutes?"

He sighed heavily. "The microwave is broken," he admitted. "And so is the oven," he added when she was about to mention that.

She looked over her shoulder at the appliances in question, the former set into the cabinets above the latter. "They look brand-new," she said as she turned back around again.

"Yeah, well, whoever built this place obviously cut corners on the appliances, because none of them work. But trust me, food like this tastes great cold."

Kendall smiled. "In other words, you've been eating your meals cold all week because you can't figure out how the microwave or stove work."

His back went up at that—figuratively *and* literally.

"No, I've been eating my meals cold because the microwave and stove *don't* work."

She gazed at him with an expression he couldn't decipher, then stood and picked up both their plates. She strode over to the microwave, set one plate on the stovetop as she opened the door and inserted one, then picked up the other and put it in beside the first. Then she looked at the keypad—which Matthias knew was completely incomprehensible to anyone except the rocket scientist who designed it—punched a few buttons with a beep-boop-beep and the microwave suddenly came alive.

He rose from his chair and crossed the kitchen to where Kendall stood. "How did you do that?" he demanded. "That thing hasn't worked since I got here."

"Well, it's fine now," she said. Then, with another little smile he wasn't quite sure how to figure out, she asked, "What else have you been having trouble with?"

"Why do you assume I've been having trouble with anything else?"

"Well, you did just mention that none of the appliances work."

"Right." He'd forgotten about that. He thought Kendall was insinuating that he had problems with small appliances. Which was completely ridiculous. He was, after all, a captain of industry. Now, if someone would just promote him to colonel of technology, he'd be all set.

He pointed over his shoulder, at the most pressing of his concerns. "The coffeemaker," he said.

She nodded knowingly. "I should have figured that out when you cooked up that bogus contract problem to trick me into bringing you coffee."

"I never—"

But she ignored him, only smiling more sweetly, as if in sympathy. "Poor Matthias. Not getting his morning coffee every day. It's a wonder you're not a drooling mess."

"Drooling mess?" he echoed. "I've never been a drooling mess. Over coffee or anything else."

"Of course you haven't."

He eyed her narrowly but said nothing. Hey, he knew he wasn't a slave to caffeine. He could quit any time he wanted. Caffeine addicts were weak. He was strong. Hell, there were days when he didn't even go near a Starbucks. He just, you know, couldn't remember the last one, that was all. Besides, real caffeine junkies drank cheap, grocery store coffee, and they drank it all day long. Matthias bought only the premium gourmet blends, and he drank only in the morning. Except on days when he needed a little extra something to get him through the afternoon. Hey, he could afford it. He still looked good. He was still healthy. Besides, there had been plenty of studies that said it was good for you. Plus he had all those issues with his father, and coffee helped take the sting out of those.

Ah, hell. What were they talking about?

"Then I guess you don't care that I have a coffeemaker like that myself," Kendall said, "and know how to fix it. If there is, in fact, anything wrong with it," she added in a way that he knew was meant to ruffle him.

It did.

"It doesn't work," he repeated, more emphatically this time. "I've done everything. Even the clock on it is wrong."

She patted him on the shoulder—something that sent a strange ripple of warmth through him—and crossed to the counter where the coffeemaker sat. Mocking him. Again, she pressed some buttons that made a couple of quick beeps. Then she pushed the big red button Matthias hadn't wanted to push himself, fearing it might trigger a nuclear strike over North Korea, and a little green light came on. But there was nothing to indicate the machine was working, no whirring of the grinder, no hiss of water as it heated, no gurgle of coffee as it dripped into the carafe.

"See?" he said. "It doesn't work."

"I set the timer for you," she told him, sidestepping his insistence that it didn't work. And it didn't work, Matthias was sure of that. "As long as you fill it with coffee and water every night, it'll start brewing at six-thirty in the morning."

He gaped at her. "How did you do that?"

She pointed to the little green light. "I set the clock to the correct time, then pushed the button that says, 'Timer.' The machine walks you through the steps after that."

Matthias hooked his hands on his hips and said nothing, only stared at Kendall in wonder, trying to figure out how the hell he was supposed to manage for the rest of his life if she was working for someone else. Because he had no choice but to admit then that he needed Kendall. *Really* needed her. What was beginning to scare him was that he was starting to suspect it wasn't only in the office where he had that need.

She smiled at him and extended her hand. "Okay, give it to me," she said, her voice tinted with laughter.

He shook his head in confusion. "What are you talking about?"

"Your new BlackBerry," she said. "The one you brought to the hotel earlier this week. I'll program it for you."

Damn, he thought. She *would* ask about that now. "It's not necessary," he told her.

She arched her brows in surprise. "You programmed it yourself?"

"Not exactly."

"Then give it to me and I'll do it for you."

He expelled an exasperated sound. "I can't."

"Why not?"

"Because it's at the bottom of Lake Tahoe."

Kendall looked at him in disbelief for a second, then she started to laugh. It was a nice laugh, Matthias thought. Full and uninhibited without being an obnoxious bray. He tried to remember the last time he'd heard Kendall laugh…and realized he never had. Not until this evening. She'd always been so serious at work. So pragmatic and professional. So enterprising and efficient. He'd always thought she was so straitlaced. So somber. It had never occurred to him that there was a woman lurking beneath her gender-neutral attire.

He watched her as she made her way back to the microwave to remove their now-warmed dinners. She was dressed as she always dressed for work—dark trousers, pale shirt, her hair pinned up on her head. But she was more relaxed now than she'd been when she worked for him. She smiled more. Laughed. Spoke to him familiarly. Called him Matthias. When she wasn't working for him, she was…different. Softer. Warmer. More approachable.

He began to feel a little warmer himself as he watched her carry their plates back to the table. Though not particularly soft, he realized with no small amount of surprise. He wondered what she'd do if he…approached.

"The steak formerly known as tartare," she said as she set his plate back on the table with a flourish. "Have at it."

Matthias smiled at her wording. *Have at it* could mean anything. And there were a lot of *its* he wanted to have. Fortunately, he and Kendall had a nice long leisurely evening ahead of them.

* * *

Kendall shook her head as she watched Matthias fiddle with a knob on the telescope, wondering what had come over him this week to make him so...so...so...

Human.

Tonight, he'd been... She smiled as a word came to her. She tried to push it away, so wildly inappropriate a description for him was it, but it wouldn't budge. There was just nothing else that was as accurate. Tonight he had been...*adorable*. All evening long. Never in her wildest dreams would she have thought she would use such an adjective to describe him. When she'd been working for him, he'd been a lot of things—gruff, focused, no-nonsense, intense—but never, ever adorable.

The closest she'd ever seen him come to being soft had been when he'd returned from this very lodge two months ago, after seeing his brother Luke for the first time in years. For a few days after his return, Matthias had seemed distant and distracted and, well, soft. But the softness had still been tempered with an edge, thanks to whatever had happened between the two men while they were here. They'd even brawled at one point over something. Although Matthias hadn't confided in Kendall what the fight had been about, he'd come back from that trip with a black eye that she'd naturally asked him about.

But even with all the changes that had come over him on that occasion—as temporary as they'd been—he hadn't seemed like a normal human being, any more than he ever seemed like a normal human being. He'd still been a powerful force to be reckoned with.

Tonight, though, that force was a soothing breeze. Just like the one rolling off the lake that nudged a stray strand of hair into Kendall's eyes. She brushed it back as she continued to watch him by the telescope, tucking it behind her ear, though, instead of bothering with trying to poke it back into the bun. By now, several such strands of hair had escaped and blew freely about her face. Short of freeing her hair and starting all over again, there wasn't much she could do about them. Not to mention there was something about the languid, peaceful evening—and okay, something about Matthias, too—that prevented her from wanting to be her usual buttoned-up self.

The broad deck stretched along the length of the back of the house, dotted here and there by sturdy wooden furniture and the occasional potted greenery. The sun hung low over the mountains behind them, spilling a wide, watery trail over the lake as it left the sky, bisecting the rippling water with a shimmer of gold. The temperature had dropped with the sun, tumbling from the eighties into the sixties, and she knew that, with full nightfall, it would go lower still. She wished she'd thought to wear a jacket. But then, she hadn't planned on leaving the hotel, had she?

Which was ironic, she thought now, because suddenly she didn't feel like going back to it.

It was just surprisingly pleasant being with Matthias now, when they were on more equal footing. No, she wasn't a corporate bigwig or hotshot industrialist, as he was. Not yet, anyway. But neither was she his assistant anymore. She could speak to him as an equal now, and did. What was nice was that he spoke to her as an equal, too.

But then she realized that wasn't exactly right, either. Because equals in business spoke to each other about business. And she and Matthias hadn't even touched on that tonight. Over dinner, they'd discussed Lake Tahoe and the lodge, the small town in Washington state where Kendall had grown up, Matthias's favorite dog when he was a boy, and how they'd both been high achievers throughout school. The sort of things people talked about when they were getting to know each other. Personally, not professionally.

"Okay, here we go," he said now, drawing her attention back to the matter at hand. "I found Venus. Come have a look."

Kendall drained the last of her wine and set her empty glass on a table next to his, then covered the half-dozen steps to where he stood by the telescope.

"You'll see it better once the sun has completely set," he added, "but even now, it's a beautiful sight to behold."

When she came to a stop beside him, he moved to one side, far enough that she would have room to look through the telescope, but still close enough that he could give her instructions, or a hand, if she needed one.

"Look through here," he said, pointing to a piece that jutted up from the enormous scope.

The thing must magnify a billion times, she thought.

"And you can focus in and out with this," he added, pointing to a knob next to the one he'd been turning to find the planet. He looked at her and smiled. "It's amazing the detail you get with this thing. When I look at the moon at night, it's like if I just stretched out far enough, I could fill my hand with moondust."

Fill my hand with moondust, Kendall repeated to herself, marveling at the phrase. Had Matthias actually said that? It was just so…so…so un-Matthias.

He seemed to realize that, too, because he suddenly looked uncomfortable. His gaze, which had been focused on hers, ricocheted off, and he began to look at everything on the deck except her. Finally, his focus lit on something behind her, and he pointed in that direction.

"Our glasses are empty," he said. "I'll open another bottle of wine." Then, still not looking directly at her, he dipped his head toward the telescope and said, "Enjoy the view. I'll be right back."

She took him at his word, but instead of enjoying the view through the scope, she instead enjoyed the view of Matthias as he strode over to collect their glasses, then made his way back into the lodge. His shirttail flapped in the breeze, rising at one point to give her a lovely view of a surprisingly nice derriere. Since it had generally been covered by a suit jacket whenever she was around him, she'd never had the chance to notice what a nice tush Matthias had. Or maybe she just hadn't allowed herself to notice, because she was working for him. Now, however, she noticed.

Boy howdy, did she notice.

Almost as if he'd heard the thought forming in her brain, Matthias spun quickly around and caught her ogling him. Heat flooded her face at being caught in such a flagrant position, and she waited for the icy look she was sure he'd shoot her way. But the look he gave her wasn't icy. In fact, it was kind of hot. For a moment, his expression didn't change. Then, gradually, an almost invisible smile curled his lips. The kind of smile he didn't want anyone to see. The kind of smile someone who knew him well—like Kendall—couldn't miss. Then it was gone, and he was turning again to make his way back inside the lodge.

But something in his smile lingered, even after he was gone. And it lingered inside Kendall. A thrill of warmth that had sparked in her belly when she first saw his smile, then gradually eased through her entire system, warming her even as the breeze off the lake began to grow cool.

Too much to drink, she decided. She and Matthias both had obviously overindulged on the wine. Funny, though, how she'd never considered two glasses of wine—spread out over two hours, with dinner—overindulging before.

Absently, she curled her arms over her midsection—because she was cold, she told herself, in spite of the warmth spreading through her, and not because she was trying to hold the feeling inside a little longer. She looked up at the bright speck in the sky with her naked eye, then bent toward the eyepiece of the telescope. It took her a moment to get in the right position, but eventually, she found what she was looking for.

Wow, she thought when she saw the yellow planet streaked with bits of orange and pink. It really *was* gorgeous. But she was still surprised that Matthias would think so, too. That he would even care there were planets up there. Looking at the sky just seemed like such a frivolous thing for him to do. That he'd been spending his evenings at the lodge out here on the deck, contemplating the mysteries of the universe, instead of in the amply equipped office getting work done, spoke volumes. And it wasn't in a language he'd ever been able to master before—that of leisure enjoyment.

Something warm and heavy slipped over her shoulders then, and she glanced up from the telescope to find Matthias settling a jacket, clearly one of his, over her shoulders.

He smiled at what must have been her obvious surprise at the gesture and said, "The temperature's dropping. I don't want you to get cold."

There was certainly no chance of that happening,

Kendall thought, as long as he looked at her the way he was looking at her now. She smiled gratefully and murmured her thanks, then pressed her eye to the eyepiece of the telescope once again.

"So what do you think?" he asked.

"You're right," she told him. "It's as if you could just reach right out and touch it."

"When it gets a little darker, I'll see if I can find Jupiter, too," he told her. "It's even more incredible. You can actually see the big red spot with this thing."

Kendall pulled her head back and looked at Matthias again. In the few minutes he'd been inside, the evening had grown noticeably darker, and now the flicker of candlelight danced in his hair, setting little gold fires amid the dark tresses. He must have lit the ones scattered about the tables and the railing while she was so rapt over the image of Venus. His gaze fixed intently on hers as he extended a glass of wine toward her, and she took it without really paying attention, automatically lifting it to her lips for a sip. It tasted different from the last glass, its flavor smoother, more mellow, more potent. Or maybe, she thought, it was just Matthias who was suddenly all those things. She'd better pace herself, or he'd go right to her head.

"So," he said, the word coming out slowly and softly, "how are things going with the new job? Do you like OmniTech so far?"

Kendall was surprised he would ask. Not just because of the whole former employer-employee thing, but because the evening had just been so pleasant and enjoyable with the absence of any talk that was work-related. Still, she knew Matthias wouldn't have asked if he didn't expect an answer. An honest one, at that.

"Actually," she said, her own reply coming out even slower and more softly than his, "so far, it's not exactly what I expected."

His expression changed not at all, but he asked, "How so?"

She shrugged, nudging back another strand of hair that blew into her face and pulling his jacket more snugly around herself. "Well, for one thing, Stephen's idea of orientation seems to be asking me a lot of questions about my old position at Barton Limited and dodging any questions *I* ask about my *new* position at OmniTech."

She waited for a smug *I told you so,* but Matthias's reply was instead a very careful, "I see."

Even though he didn't ask for more information, she found herself continuing anyway. "Orientation will be over after tomorrow, and I know almost nothing about Omni-Tech, save the history of the company and its mission statement and where its national and international offices are located and—" She halted abruptly. "Anything I could find out myself by an online search."

Matthias sipped his wine, but again said nothing, just waited for her to continue, should she want to. The sky behind him was smudged dark blue, the fat full moon hovering over his left shoulder. The only other light came from the candles flickering inside the hurricane globes on the tables, but it was enough to allow her to see his expression. Unfortunately, she couldn't tell by his expression what he was thinking, and that bothered her a lot. Not that she wanted to know what he thought about her situation with OmniTech, but because she wanted to know what he thought about *her.* If he considered her naive for not realizing what he had about Stephen DeGallo, or foolish for having disregarded his warning, or ridiculous for clinging to the idea that she had made the right choice.

Especially since she was no longer clinging to that idea. With every new meeting she had with Stephen, her suspicions about the man and his motives grew stronger. His having blown off their dinner meeting tonight—regardless of his reason for doing so—had only cemented her fear that what Matthias had told her was true. Stephen DeGallo had hired her because he'd hoped she would give him insight into Matthias's business. Which, of course, she would never do. Her job performance at Barton Limited was pertinent to Stephen only in so far as assuring him she had achieved enough experience to perform the job for which he had hired her, that her record was stellar, and that she was committed to her professional obligations. Period.

Now that he had realized she had no intention of playing corporate spy, he was no longer interested. She wouldn't be surprised if, before her alleged orientation even ended tomorrow afternoon, he manufactured some reason to let her go. Thanks to reorganization, the position for which he'd had her in mind was no longer viable. Or he'd discovered something in her work history that presented a conflict of interest. Oh, he'd find some way to make it sound plausible. He might even give her a generous severance package—though she doubted it. But there was certainly reason to believe her new position at OmniTech wouldn't be hers for long.

She looked at Matthias. "You were right," she said, forcing herself to admit the truth. "I think the only reason Stephen hired me was because he assumed I would share what I know about Barton Limited with him."

Matthias eyed her warily now. "Did he ask you about the Perkins contract?"

She shook her head. "Not specifically, no. Not yet, anyway. But he did ask an awful lot of questions about you and the company. I wouldn't be surprised if the particulars of the Perkins contract was next on his to-do list."

"And what did you tell him about Barton Limited?" Matthias asked, his voice revealing nothing of what he might be thinking about.

She smiled. "I told him about the history of the company and its mission statement and where its national and international offices are located. You know. Anything he could discover by doing an online search."

Matthias smiled back. "That's my girl."

Something about the way he said it, so soft and intimate, sent a ripple of awareness shimmying through her unlike anything she had ever felt before. The breeze chose that moment to pull another strand of hair from the knot at the back of her head and nudge it across her eyes. She started to reach up to brush it away, but Matthias intercepted her, dipping his index finger beneath the disobedient tresses and brushing them back from her forehead. Then he surprised her even more by moving his hand to the clip that held the mass of hair in place and pulling it free.

"You might as well just leave it loose," he told her as he completed the action. "The wind is only going to pick up as the evening goes on."

Which, Kendall thought, was all the more reason to keep her hair anchored. Matthias obviously thought differently. Because as her hair tumbled down around her shoulders, he dragged his fingers through it the way a stylist would, pushing it back over her shoulders, then forward again, then back, as if he wasn't sure how he liked it best. But where a stylist would keep his touches dispassionate and economical, Matthias took his time, stroking the straight, shoulder-length tresses again and again. Kendall finally had to reach up and circle his wrist with her fingers to stop him. When she did, he immediately halted, his gaze connecting fiercely with hers.

For a moment, neither of them spoke, neither of them moved, neither even seemed to breathe. Matthias dropped his gaze from Kendall's eyes to her mouth, then looked into her eyes again. She felt her lips part almost of their own volition, though whether it was because she intended to say something, or for another reason entirely, she wasn't sure. The moment stretched taut, and still neither spoke or moved. Then, for one scant, insane instant, it almost seemed as if he were dipping his head toward hers, tilting it slightly, as if he intended to…

Kiss her? Kendall thought frantically. Oh, surely not.

But her heart began to hammer in her chest all the same, and heat flared in her belly, and her pulse rate quickened, and her entire body caught fire, and then…and then…

And then Matthias suddenly, but gently, pulled his hand from her grasp and leaned back again, and the moment full of…whatever it had been full of…evaporated. He looked down at his glass and lifted it to his lips, filling his mouth with the dark red wine, savoring it for a moment before swallowing. Kendall was still too keyed up and confused by what she was feeling to say anything, so she watched him instead, noting how his strong throat worked over the swallow, feeling warmth spread through her belly as if she were the one who had drunk deeply from her glass.

When Matthias looked at her again, his expression was bland and unreadable, as if there had been nothing about the last few minutes that was any different from the millions of minutes that had preceded them. As if wanting to emphasize that, he asked a question guaranteed to dispel any strange sensations that might be lingering.

"So what do you plan to do about Stephen?"

Kendall wished she had an answer for all the questions—both spoken and unspoken—that had arisen this evening, but most especially for that one. Her future, at the moment, was shakier and more open than it had ever been before. And she wasn't the sort of person who found the unknown exciting. On the contrary, she couldn't function if she didn't have a thorough, well-thought-out plan. The only plan she had at the moment, though, was to have another sip of her wine. Which she did.

Then, "I don't know," she finally said. "I feel like Stephen hired me under false pretenses, and I don't want to work for OmniTech if that's the case. I'd like to be hired on the merit of my knowledge and potential, not because I might have juicy gossip."

"You could resign," Matthias said.

She studied him in silence for a moment, wondering why he'd made the suggestion he had. Was it because he wanted to be proven right? Or was he looking out for Kendall's best interests? Or was it simply because he wanted to stick it to Stephen DeGallo?

Not long ago, she would have assumed it was either the first or last of those reasons. Now, however, she couldn't help thinking maybe he really did want to help Kendall do what was best for herself.

"It will probably be a moot point," she said. "If he decides I'm not going to be beneficial to him in the way he first thought, I wouldn't be surprised if he manufactures some excuse to let me go."

She raised a shoulder and let it drop, hoping the half shrug hid the turmoil roiling inside her. What was weird was that the turmoil was less a result of the prospect of being unemployed, and more the result of the way Matthias continued to look at her.

He dropped his gaze into his glass again, swirling the dark wine around the sides of the bowl in thoughtful concentration. "Well, if you do decide to resign," he began, "or if Stephen is stupid enough to let you go, I have a position at Barton Limited that needs filling." He glanced up at Kendall again, fixing his gaze on hers. "If you think you'd be interested. You'd be perfect for it."

For some reason, his offer of her old job back didn't rankle her as much as it had before. Maybe because this time he wasn't being such an arrogant jackass about it. No, this time, his tone was solicitous, his body language inquisitive. This time, it was indeed an offer, not an order. But Kendall was no more interested in accepting it now than she had been before. She still wanted—needed—more than to be Matthias Barton's assistant. She was too smart and too ambitious, and she wanted to do more—with her life and herself.

"Matthias, I can't be your assistant anymore," she told him. "We've been through this. I need something that will challenge me to be the best that I can be."

"I'm not offering you your old job back," he told her. "I'm offering you a new one."

Kendall wasn't sure if she should be suspicious or not. Ultimately, she decided on being cautious. "What kind of position?"

He turned toward the deck railing and leaned over to

prop his arms on it, then gazed up at the moon as he spoke. "There's no title for it yet. But I'm getting ready to acquire a technology company that's been failing due to mismanagement and carelessness. I'm going to need someone to work side by side with me getting it whipped into shape."

Kendall told herself not to make anything of his body language—that he was looking at the moon and might be, figuratively anyway, offering her something that didn't exist—and consider what he was saying. "Tell me more about the company," she asked carefully.

He did, describing its rise and fall and the problems that had led to its faltering. She nodded as he spoke, turning over in her mind the possibilities and potential, and the various avenues they could take to put the company back on its feet. When Matthias finished, she asked, "What's the salary and benefits for this position?"

"Quadruple what you made as my assistant," he told her.

Her eyebrows shot up at that. That was two times more than the position at OmniTech.

"Full medical and dental," he added, "contributions to an IRA and 401(k). And, if you want, we can talk stock options."

"I want," she said readily.

By now he had straightened again and was lifting his glass to his mouth. But he stopped so abruptly when Kendall said what she did that some of the ruby wine spilled over onto his hand. Hastily, he took the glass in his other hand and tried to shake the wine from his fingers, then looked around for something to wipe the rest of it off. Kendall, always prepared, pulled a clean handkerchief from her trouser pocket and handed it to him. He set his glass down, wiped his hand clean, then, out of habit, she guessed, deftly tucked the scrap of cotton into his own pocket.

When he looked at her again, he seemed agitated about something. But all he said was, "Then let's talk."

Kendall met his gaze levelly. "Okay. I'm listening."

Seven

The coffee shop where Stephen had scheduled their "morning meeting," which he'd deemed "unavoidable" on a Saturday because Kendall's "orientation" had "fallen behind" this week—yeah, Stephen, since some people blew off "essential dinner meetings" to instead chase after breathtaking blondes—was located a couple of blocks away from the inn. But it was every bit as quaint and charming. Even though it was early—and also *Saturday,* in case Kendall hadn't mentioned that part—there were a number of people out and about, ambling down the walkways, waiting for the shops to open and sipping their morning lattes. But, unlike Kendall, who was dressed in her usual business trousers and shirt—in this case beige for the former and cream for the latter—everyone else sported vacation clothes, mostly shorts and T-shirts or loose cotton dresses coupled with sneakers or sandals. Because they, unlike Kendall, didn't have to work today. On account of it was Saturday. In case she hadn't mentioned that part.

She looked longingly down at her pointy-toed, three-inch ivory pumps, then at the beat-up Birkenstock sandals on a woman passing by, and she sighed. Someday, she thought, she was going to be the big cheese at her own successful corporation. And the first policy she planned to put in place was a Casual Friday. Then she'd add a Casual Thursday. And a Casual Wednesday, Tuesday and Monday, too. And then she'd decree that no work ever took place on the weekend.

She knew her business philosophy was an unconventional one. Most corporate big shots had gotten where they were by working overtime, downtime, double time and time and a half. She knew it was traditional to keep employees toeing a conservative line in all things business-related. And she knew power suits made a more imposing impression than well, beat-up Birkenstock sandals. But she also knew that the *real* secret to success was loving what you did for a living.

And Kendall loved big business. She just wasn't that crazy about all its trappings. She didn't think the image was as important as other people did. As far as she was concerned, actions spoke louder than power suits. She would rather have a force of casually dressed, happy, productive employees working for her than she would a bunch of polished corporate drones. It wasn't enough to be smart and energetic in today's business world. Creativity was absolutely essential. And creative people were *not* a suit-wearing tribe. So Kendall was going to cut her workforce a little slack.

She toed off one pointy-toed high heel and let it drop to the sidewalk. And she would cut herself some slack, too.

Matthias hadn't had a title or description yet for the job he'd offered her, but she wasn't worried. No matter what it was, she would do it well. She would play by his rules for as long as it took to get the business off the ground, and then she would tailor it to her policies and procedures and put her own personal stamp on it. Matthias, for all his conservative bluster, had always been an open-minded and farsighted businessman. It was part of what had made him so successful. He would allow—no, expect—Kendall to be her own woman with whatever he gave her to direct. And she couldn't wait to get started.

As if cued by the thought, Stephen DeGallo turned the corner just then, catching Kendall's eye and raising a hand in greeting. He was having a Casual Saturday, she noticed, wearing faded jeans with a brightly patterned tiki shirt and, she noted with some wistfulness, sandals.

"You didn't have to dress for work," he said by way of a greeting as he sat down across from her.

Kendall eyed him with what she hoped looked like terseness, since terse was suddenly how she felt. "Well, since we're *supposed* to be *working*," she said meaningfully, "I dressed for work."

"But it's Saturday," he said with a smile. Then he looked past her and waved to catch a waiter's attention. "You don't have to be all buttoned-up and battened down. Live a little."

Yeah, like you did last night, huh, Stephen? Kendall had to bite her lip to keep the words from tumbling out. Instead, she was the picture of politeness when she asked, "What happened to you last night?"

He looked genuinely puzzled. "Last night?"

She nodded. "We were supposed to have a dinner

meeting. To discuss which OmniTech health-care plan would be best for me."

He shook his head. "No, we're doing that this afternoon."

Kendall turned her head and tugged lightly on an earring. "No, it was supposed to be last night, Stephen. In fact, when we parted ways yesterday afternoon after our session on the new sweetheart agreement you made with one of the subsidiaries I'd be working with, you distinctly said, 'I'll see you at six-thirty.' But I waited twenty minutes, and you never showed."

He looked a little taken aback, presumably by her tone, which, she had to admit, wasn't the sort of voice one normally used with an employer. Particularly a brand-new one. No, it was more the tone of voice one used with a dog who had just peed on the carpet.

His eyes went flinty. Then he smiled, a gesture that fell well short of making him look happy. "I meant six-thirty *tonight*," he said.

"No, you meant Friday," she countered with all confidence. "I don't make mistakes like that."

"Neither do I."

"You did last night," Kendall told him pointedly. "Or maybe you just found yourself…preoccupied by a better prospect. A blond prospect."

His smile disappeared, and his eyes hardened even more. "What I do in my private time is none of your business, Kendall."

"It is if it affects my job."

He expelled a soft sound of undisguised contempt. "What job?" he demanded. "You're fired, effective immediately."

Not that Kendall minded, since it would save her the trouble of resigning and get her out of OmniTech more quickly, but she felt compelled to ask, "On what grounds?" Mostly because she didn't want to leave any loose threads hanging. And, okay, also because she wanted to goad him.

"What grounds?" he asked incredulously. "How about insubordination for starters? You're also completely unsuited to the position I hired you for."

Ridiculous, she thought. She was perfect for the job of vice president. And in a few years, once she got her legs, she'd be perfect for the job of CEO. After that, she wasn't sure, but she might take over the universe. At the moment, she felt perfectly capable—she was that confident of her abilities.

Evidently, Stephen didn't have such an inflated opinion of her, however, because he continued, "You're also withdrawn and uncooperative, and you're *not* a team player."

Kendall nodded at this. By his definition of those words, he was right, and she told him so. "In other words, I'm ethical to the point that I won't roll over on my former employer and tell you all his best-kept business secrets."

Stephen's mouth shut tight at that, but he said nothing.

"That's why you hired me, isn't it, Stephen? Because you thought I'd speak freely about Matthias Barton. You thought I'd make you privy to all his personal quirks and habits and reveal the details of any of his dealings that I might have been in on."

For a moment, Stephen said nothing. Then he sneered at her and said, "As if Matthias Barton would allow his *secretary* to be in on any of his dealings. I don't know what I was thinking to assume a nobody like you would have any insight into a rival corporation."

Kendall smiled sweetly. "For one thing, Stephen, secretaries are the backbone of any good business. They're not nobodies. For another thing, you're wrong. I know more about Matthias's business than Matthias does. He'd tell you himself he couldn't operate without me. So much so, that he's offered me a job. An executive position," she added confidently, even though she was confident of no such thing. Matthias had made clear that the job—whatever it was—*was* important. Essential. Valuable. And it was hers, the moment she was free of Stephen DeGallo.

Which was going to happen more quickly than she initially thought.

"You can't fire me, Stephen," she told him as she stood. "I quit." Much better than resigning, she thought. As she slung her purse over her shoulder, she added, "Thanks for the coffee. And the reality check. I assure you both were *much* appreciated."

And then she turned and strode confidently down the sidewalk, back toward the Timber Lake Inn. She had an unexpected day off, she thought with a smile. Well, okay, maybe not all *that* unexpected. She'd planned to tell Stephen this morning that she wouldn't be coming to work for OmniTech, and she'd been fairly sure he would terminate her on the spot. She'd just thought it would go a little more smoothly, that was all. She truly hadn't meant for things to end as abruptly as they had, or with as much chilliness.

But Stephen *had* deliberately skipped their meeting last night, something that had illustrated his disregard for her as both a person and an employee. And he *had* hired her under false pretenses to begin with. It hadn't exactly been a situation that lent itself to air kisses and toodle-oos. If she'd been too pushy or blunt—

Her steps slowed and her back straightened. She smiled. If she'd been too pushy and blunt, then it just meant she was a solid businesswoman. Any man who'd been pushy and blunt would have been applauded and called assertive and candid. So she was going to applaud herself, too.

Boy, what a couple of days for changes and epiphanies, Kendall thought. So far, she'd accepted a new power job, resigned from an old dubious job, told her sleazy ex-employer what a sleazy ex-employer he was, discovered what an assertive businesswoman *she* was, and now she could go back to her hotel and—

She halted in her tracks, her confidence fleeing completely. Because she realized then that her hotel wasn't her hotel anymore. Stephen DeGallo wasn't going to foot the bill for her room now that she wasn't in his employ. And he'd probably cancel her return ticket to San Francisco, not to mention the rental car. And with it being the peak of the summer tourist season, finding a flight *or* car right away might prove to be a bit daunting.

She was going to have to check out of the Timber Lake Inn. She had nowhere else to go and no way to get there.

She sighed and gave her forehead a good mental smack. So much for being the assertive, candid businesswoman who could take over the universe at will. In a matter of hours, Kendall was going to be living on the streets.

Matthias was reading a political thriller he'd found in one of the spare bedrooms when he heard the front doorbell ring. He set it facedown on the sofa and went to answer, automatically brushing the dust from his jeans and pin-striped, untucked oxford, even though the house wasn't old enough to have accumulated any dust, and even though, if it did, Mandy or Mindy or Maureen or whatever the hell the caretaker's name was would make quick work of it.

Mary, he remembered as he stepped into the foyer.

Mary, who had seemed strangely familiar for some reason, even though, at the moment, Matthias couldn't even remember what she looked like. For all he knew, it was she who was at the front door right now. He hadn't seen her since the day of his arrival. Not that he'd expected to. He wasn't even sure if she lived here in Hunter's Landing. But something about her had made him think she had a vested interest in the house and would check on it from time to time to make sure none of the Seven Samurai was trashing the place with wild parties and wilder behavior.

Even though the days of their trashing anything—like the furniture they'd nailed to the ceiling in the dorm their freshman year—had long since passed. These days the Seven Samurai, in addition to no longer being seven, were no longer the soldier of fortune types they'd fancied themselves when they'd assumed the nickname for the group as young men. They'd all made their fortunes in one way or another, and now they were all too busy trying to protect those fortunes and make them grow larger to have time for wild parties and wilder behavior.

And why that realization made Matthias's mouth turn down in consternation, he couldn't have said.

But his mouth turned up again when he opened the front door, and his step felt lighter—even if he was standing still—when he saw that it wasn't the caretaker who stood on the other side, but Kendall.

Her appearance surprised him. Not so much her appearance on his doorstep, but rather her *appearance* on his doorstep. She was dressed in the kind of thing he'd never seen her wear before—blue jeans that were faded to the point of being torn in places, and a pale lavender T-shirt that was brief enough to allow a glimpse of creamy flesh between its hem and the waistband of her jeans. Even more surprising than Kendall's appearance, however, was her luggage's appearance, since, by virtue of its appearance, it was apparent that it would be visiting, too. It was scattered about her feet in a way that made it look as if she'd just dropped it there in frustration before ringing the bell.

She sounded frustrated, too, when she said, by way of a greeting, "Can I ask you a favor?"

Matthias tried to tear his gaze away from that very alluring strip of naked flesh…and failed miserably. Still gazing at the hem of her shirt, he mentally willed it to leap up again the way it had—all too briefly—when she'd shoved her hands into her back pockets. And somehow he conjured the presence of mind to reply to her question. Unfortunately, that reply was a very distracted, "Huh?"

She shifted her weight from one foot to the other, an action which, although not the one he was mentally willing her to complete, nevertheless had the desired result. For another scant second, that band of naked flesh widened, causing the heavens to open up and a chorus of angels to sing, "Hallelujah, hoo-ah."

"Can I ask you a favor?" Kendall said again.

But she said it without moving her body, unfortunately, so her shirt stayed in place. Then again, that at least allowed Matthias to be coherent enough to answer her question this time. Kind of. At least he got out an "Mmm-hmm" that sounded vaguely affirmative in nature. The problem was, by then, he couldn't remember what the question was that he was answering.

His reply seemed to be fine for Kendall, though, because

she continued, "Would it be possible for me to crash here for a couple of days?"

The question was unexpected enough to command a much larger chunk of his attention. So unexpected, in fact, that he wouldn't have been more surprised if Kendall had just asked him if it would be possible for him to pull the Empire State Building out of his pocket. Then again, the way he was beginning to feel watching the comings and goings of her shirttail, that might not be such an unreasonable request in a few more minutes.

He managed to cover his reaction well, though—he hoped. And through some herculean effort, he also managed to bring his gaze back up to her face. "Problems at the inn?" he asked.

She shook her head. "Problems at OmniTech."

Hey, that sounded promising, he thought. "What kind of problems?"

"I sort of quit. Effective immediately."

He was wrong. That wasn't promising. It was perfect.

Before he could say anything more, she hurried on, "But I sort of didn't take into consideration until too late the fact that, by quitting, I was also ending any reason for Stephen to pay my hotel bill. In the time it took me to walk from the café where we had our morning meeting back to my room, the lock had already been changed on my door. The only reason I was able to get my stuff out was because housekeeping showed up, and the housekeeper was nice enough to let me change my clothes and pack while she was in there cleaning."

Thank God for small favors, Matthias thought. Inescapably, his gaze had dropped to her midsection again when he'd noticed—how could he miss it?—that as Kendall had spoken, she had used a lot of hand gestures, and the hem of her little T-shirt rose and fell with every one, once even high enough to allow him a peek at a truly spectacular navel. So spectacular, in fact, that he enjoyed a quick impression of dragging a line of openmouthed kisses across her flat abdomen before dipping his tongue into the elegant little cleft for a taste....

Until he remembered it was Kendall's navel he was tasting in his fantasy. Kendall, he reminded himself emphatically. This was *Kendall* he was thinking about, for God's sake. *Kendall*'s midsection. And *Kendall*'s navel. All of them were strictly off-limits because... Because... Because...

Well, because she was Kendall, Matthias told himself. That was why. A trusted employee. A trusted employee he didn't want to compromise with some kind of messy workplace involvement. A trusted employee with an excellent work record. A trusted employee with strong business ethics and sound professional judgment.

A trusted employee with silky dark blond hair that was tumbling free around her shoulders in a way that made him want to reach out and touch it. A trusted employee with enormous green eyes a man could drown in. A trusted employee with a luscious navel he really, really wanted to taste.

"So if the offer of that new position is still open," his luscious, tasty, trusted employee said now, "I'd like to come back to work for you."

The word that should have registered most in that sentence was *work*. But Matthias's brain had gotten so caught up on *position* that it never quite made the leap to *work*. And the position that came to mind just then, although it definitely involved Kendall, had absolutely nothing to do with work. Well, okay, maybe there would have to be a little work involved—it was kind of an unusual position—but that work would have definitely been a labor of lo—

Lust, he hastily corrected himself. A labor of lust.

"Matthias?"

His name, spoken in her voice, a voice so rife with concern, made him push the thoughts out of his head completely. "What?" he asked.

She eyed him curiously. "Is everything…okay?"

He nodded. "Yeah, fine," he said with some distraction. "I was reading when you rang the bell, and I guess my mind just hasn't caught up with the rest of me."

Actually, that wasn't true, he knew. His mind had not only caught up, it had raced right past him and was now in an entirely different time zone. The Navel Zone. Where time moved at a totally different pace than it did in Lake Tahoe.

"So is it okay if I crash here for a couple of days?" she asked again. "I had to change my flight back to San Francisco, and I couldn't get one out until Monday. I tried to find a room at another hotel, but all the good ones are booked solid, and—"

"It's fine, Kendall," he interrupted her. "Of course you can stay here. There's plenty of room."

Though the minute he said that, somehow, for some reason, the huge lodge suddenly felt very crowded.

"Thanks," she said, breathing a sigh of unmistakable relief.

She bent to retrieve her bags, but Matthias intercepted her, scooping up all three before she had the chance. When he looked at her again, he could tell she was surprised by the gesture. Or maybe it was just that she was usually the one doing things for him, not the other way around.

It hit Matthias then, like a two-by-four to the back of

the head, how very true that was. When she was working for him, Kendall had done so many things for him to keep him on track. Granted, that was what he paid her for, but still. What had he ever done for her in return, other than pay her wages and benefits? Yeah, there had been the Godiva chocolates for her birthday every year and the gourmet food baskets every Christmas. But those had been things he'd had his secretary order for her—and he hadn't even picked them out himself.

Then again, Kendall had never seemed to expect anything more, he told himself. Then again—again—that was no excuse for not showing his appreciation more often.

Note to self, Barton. Show Kendall a little appreciation this time around. As a reluctant afterthought, he made himself add, *And appreciate something besides her navel.*

It would be a tough job, but he was pretty sure he could do it.

She followed him up to the second floor where Matthias had a choice of guest rooms in which to house her. Not asking himself why he did it, he made his way immediately to one near the master bedroom, where he was sleeping himself. The room was furnished in varying shades of green and gold, the stout four-poster covered with a light-weight patchwork quilt, the hardwood floors broken up here and there with rag rugs. It was what Matthias had come to think of as the Rustic Room. Though it was every bit as luxurious as the rest of the house. The wide windows opened onto a thick patch of pine trees, beyond which was a spectacular view with a finger of lake on one side. At night, he thought, she could do what he'd been doing—lie in bed and listen to the wind gliding through the trees, and wait for the melancholy hoot-hoot-hoot of a solitary owl.

Hey, it wasn't as if there was much else to do around the lodge at night. At least, there hadn't been before.

"Why don't you stay more than a couple of days?" he asked impulsively as he tossed Kendall's bags onto the bed.

When he turned, he saw that she had stopped in the doorway, and she didn't look as if she planned on coming in anytime soon.

"I mean, you quit OmniTech," he pointed out unnecessarily, "and I'm not going to be coming back to San Francisco for a few more weeks. I don't expect you to report to the office before I get back myself. When was the last time you took a vacation?"

She threw him a funny look. "I just had one. Two weeks between leaving Barton Limited and going to work for OmniTech."

"Oh. Right. Well, what did you do during those two weeks?" he asked. "I bet you didn't spend them out of town, did you?"

"No," she admitted. "I did some work around my condo that I'd been putting off for a while."

"Well, there you go," Matthias said. "You need a vacation. I have a vacation home. At least for a few more weeks."

She crossed her arms over her midsection and dropped her weight to one foot. "And besides," she said, "you brought a lot of work with you from the office, and you could use someone to help out with it while you're here. Right?"

He gaped at her, shocked that she could think such a thing of him. What shocked him even more was that what she'd just accused him of had never once crossed his mind. "Of course not," he denied. "Yeah, I brought work with me, but I'm getting it done just fine by myself."

Well, except for how his laptop kept eating his files and

how he couldn't figure out how to open Excel and how every time he tried to send e-mail on the desktop in the office upstairs, a box kept popping up with all kinds of weird symbols in it that he was reasonably certain were the equivalent of digital profanity. Really bad digital profanity, too. Other than that, everything was fine.

She smiled at him in a way that made him think she knew exactly what kind of problems he was having. Then she surprised him by saying, "Okay, I'll stay a couple more days. It is a beautiful place. And I could use some downtime."

Matthias wasn't sure what to make of the ripple of pleasure that wound through him at her acceptance of his invitation. So he decided not to question it. In fact, he decided not to think about it at all. Because Kendall's smile grew broader then, and she crossed her arms in a way that made her little T-shirt ride up on her torso again, giving him another delicious glimpse at that navel. The ripple of pleasure turned into a raging tsunami at that, and he was suddenly overcome by the absolute conviction that his life would never get better than it was in that moment, standing in the same room with Kendall and her navel, knowing she would be around for a few more days.

But he was wrong. Because what she said to him after that multiplied his pleasure tenfold and nearly sent his body into paroxysms of ecstasy.

Because what she said then was, "You know, I need to run into town to pick up a few things. Why don't we look for a new BlackBerry for you while we're there? And I'll get it all nice and programmed for you, just the way you like it."

That was when Matthias knew, without doubt, that Kendall Scarborough was the only woman in the world who would ever be able to make him happy.

"But, Matthias," she added, more soberly this time, "you have to promise me you won't contact that guy in Nigeria or the woman with the Web cam."

He narrowed his eyes in confusion. "Why not?"

"Just don't. Trust me."

Strangely, he realized he already did. Implicitly. Though, thinking back on their history together, maybe that wasn't so strange after all. What was strange was that, suddenly, for some reason, he realized he also trusted Kendall in ways that went beyond the professional. But what was strangest of all was that he found himself wanting her to trust him, too. In ways that had nothing to do with the professional.

"C'mon," she said. "You'll have to drive. Let's pick up some groceries, too. I'm tired of hotel food and carryout. Let's cook tonight."

Eight

They weren't able to find a BlackBerry for Matthias in tiny Hunter's Landing. They did lots of other things there—shared a banana split at the ice-cream parlor, played air hockey at the arcade, selected fresh produce at the farmer's market and enjoyed a late-afternoon beer at the pub—but the little community was fresh out of sophisticated gadgetry by the time they arrived. Interestingly, Matthias wasn't even halfway through the banana split when he forgot all about it. And when Kendall made mention of it again halfway through the afternoon beer, he had to take a minute to remember that, oh, yeah, that was one of the reasons they'd gone into town, wasn't it? Because by then, he was enjoying himself so much with Kendall that he couldn't even remember why he'd wanted a BlackBerry in the first place.

Nor could he remember the last time he'd played air

hockey. Probably because he had played with Luke, and it had probably been one of those death matches the two of them never seemed able to avoid. With Kendall, they hadn't even kept score. Matthias couldn't remember the last time he'd had a banana split, either, and he'd certainly never shared one before, thanks to the I-got-mine mentality he'd grown up with under his father's misguided tutelage. Even the afternoon beer was unusual for Matthias. He never took time out of his day to engage in things that had no purpose other than to make the day a little nicer.

And the thing was, the day would have been nicer even without all those things, simply because Kendall was a part of it.

Why had he never realized before how much he liked having her around? he wondered as they drove back to the lodge, chatting amiably the whole way. She'd worked for him for five years—five years—and not once had it occurred to him that the reason his life was as good as it was was due in large part to Kendall's simple presence in it. All that time, he'd thought he valued her for her efficiency and organizational skills. It was only after she'd left that he'd realized she'd brought so much more to his life.

He *liked* Kendall. He liked her a lot. Not just as an employee, but as a person. As a friend. As a companion. The two of them had an easy camaraderie with each other after all these years that he hadn't even realized had developed. A give and take, an ebb and flow, an itch and scratch that was as well orchestrated and choreographed as a Broadway show. And now he understood that that camaraderie transcended their working relationship. Today, they'd enjoyed an ease of conversation Matthias didn't share with people he'd known twice as long as Kendall.

And last night, out on the deck with the telescope... That had been one of the most enjoyable evenings he'd ever had.

Even as they unpacked and put away their groceries, they spoke easily and moved in concert with each other as if they did this all the time. The preparation of dinner, too, was another perfectly executed team effort, as was the cleaning up afterward. As Matthias opened a second bottle of wine, Kendall reached into the cupboard for two fresh glasses. As he poured, she dimmed the lights, and, together, they retreated to the lodge's lush living room.

The sun was setting over the mountains, leaving the lake midnight-blue and smooth as silk. Matthias watched Kendall head for a lamp, then hesitate before turning it on. He understood. The lighting outside this time of evening was just too beautiful not to appreciate it. When she moved to the massive windows to look out on the vista, he joined her. But it wasn't the lake and mountains that drew his eye. It was Kendall's expression as she looked at them, all soft and mellow and contented. The way he felt himself.

"This place is truly gorgeous," she said.

He nodded, still looking at her. "Gorgeous," he echoed.

"I can't believe your friend had it built and isn't able to be here to enjoy it."

Matthias sighed, turning to look out at the view now. "Oh, I imagine Hunter's enjoying it, wherever he is. I think he's enjoying seeing the effect the place has on all of us. Somehow he knew all those years ago what kind of men the Seven Samurai would turn out to be."

"And what kind of men did you all turn out to be?" she asked.

Matthias inhaled a deep breath and let it out slowly. "Men who are too busy building our empires to remember why we wanted to build them in the first place. Men who work so hard, we've forgotten how to live."

But he realized as he said it that that hadn't been true of him today. Today, Matthias had forgotten all about work. Today, he'd forgotten all about empires. Today, he'd thought only about Kendall. And today, more than any other day of his life, he had *lived*. He'd lived, and he'd enjoyed living. He'd enjoyed it a lot. More, even, than work.

From the corner of his eye, he saw Kendall turn toward him, but he continued to gaze out the window, looking for…something. He wasn't sure what.

"You miss him, don't you?" she said softly.

He nodded. "It happened so quickly. By the time the doctors found the cancer, it was too late to do anything to save him."

"It must have been hard on you and your other friends."

Hard wasn't the word, Matthias thought. "Devastating," he said instead. "It tore us apart, in more ways than one. Hunter was the glue that kept us together. I think that was his gift—that he knew people. Knew what made them tick. Knew what made them behave the way they did. I mean, look at what he did for me and Luke."

"What?" Kendall asked. "I thought you guys didn't get along."

"We don't. Didn't," he immediately corrected himself. "But in college, we did. Somehow Hunter made us see past all the animosity and one-upmanship our father generated in us. Luke and I were friends—real friends—in college. But after Hunter died…"

He didn't continue. What had happened to Matthias and Luke was complicated and unsettled, and he didn't want to talk about anything complicated or unsettling tonight.

So he only said, "We all drifted apart after college. We all did well, at least professionally, but we lost each other."

He did turn to look at Kendall then. "Until now," he said, smiling. "This lodge, Hunter bringing us all here, it's getting us together again. There's going to be a reunion in September, once Jack has fulfilled his obligation to spend the month here." Although he had no idea what possessed him to do it, Matthias added, "Would you like to come back with me for that?"

Her eyes widened in surprise at the invitation. And truth be told, Matthias was surprised he'd extended it. But once said, it seemed perfectly natural. Perfectly normal. Something about having Kendall there with the friends from his past—the people who had always been more important to Matthias than anyone else—felt right.

She nodded slowly, smiling. "I'd love to come," she said. "It would be nice to meet all your old friends. And your brother, too."

Matthias wasn't sure why he did what he did next. Something about the moment, about the lodge, about the woman, just made it feel right. Dipping his head toward Kendall's, he covered her mouth with his and kissed her.

Lightly at first, gently, a part of him fearing she might pull away. But she didn't pull away. She tilted her head to the side a little, to make it easier for him, and then she kissed him back. Slowly, sweetly, almost as if she'd been expecting it, and as if she wondered what had taken him so long.

Kendall wasn't sure when the line between her and Matthias disappeared, whether it had happened just now, or during the banana split, or when she finally quit, or if it had happened years ago at a point she didn't even notice.

But when he kissed her, the way he did, she knew that line would never be back again. And then she stopped thinking about any of that, because the feelings blooming inside her, and the sensations twining through her body, were just too delicious to ignore. All she knew was that, one minute, Matthias had been looking out the window and talking about Hunter, and the next, he was surrounding her.

As he kissed her, he plucked her wineglass from her hand, and she followed his mouth with hers as he bent slightly to place both their glasses on an end table beside them. Then they were both straightening again, and he was pulling her into his arms completely, opening his mouth over hers now, tasting her deeply. She felt his hands on her back, first skimming along her spine, then curling around over her nape, then tangling in her hair. Instinctively, she raised her own hands to explore him, too, touching his rough face, his hard shoulders, his silky hair, savoring the different textures and reveling in the heat, the strength, the power she encountered beneath her fingertips.

He towered over her, seeming to touch her everywhere. Every time she inhaled, she filled her lungs with the scent of him and her mouth with the taste of him. His heart thundered against her own, the rapid beating of both mixing and mingling, until she wasn't sure which was his and which was hers. Their breathing, too, grew fierce and ragged as the kiss intensified, until Kendall felt as though their breath had also joined and become one.

One hand still tangled in her hair, he moved the other to her hip, inching it slowly downward to curve over her fanny, pushing her body forward into his. Kendall responded instinctively, rubbing her pelvis against his, sinuously, seductively, loving his growl of satisfaction in response. He moved his hand higher again, bunching the fabric of her shirt in his fist and pushing upward. She felt the cool kiss of air on her heated back with every new bit of flesh he exposed. When his fingers had crept high enough for him to realize she wasn't wearing a bra, he groaned again, splaying his fingers wide over her naked skin before deepening the kiss even more.

Thinking turnabout was fair play, Kendall dipped her hand under the hem of his shirt, too, steering her fingers over the silky swell of muscle and sinew that crisscrossed his back. Then she brought her hand forward, caressing the springy hair of his chest and the taut musculature of his torso. He was hard in all the places she was soft, angled in all the places she was curved, rough in all the places she was smooth. But his skin was as hot as hers was, and his heart beat every bit as rapidly. Their differences complemented each other, but their similarities were what brought them together. They wanted each other equally. That was enough.

She felt his hand move to her waist then, squeezing between their bodies long enough to deftly flick open the fly of her jeans and tug the zipper down. Then he was at her back again, tucking his hand into the soft denim and under the fabric of her panties, curving over her bare flesh, stroking her sensitive skin again and again and again. Heat and dampness bloomed between her legs as he stroked her, then exploded when he dipped one confident finger into the delicate cleft of her behind.

"Oh," she murmured against his mouth. "Oh, Matthias…"

But he covered her mouth again before she could say more. Not that she really knew what else she wanted to say. At the moment, she only wanted to do. Do things to and with him, and have things done to her in return.

Things she had never even allowed herself to dream about, things that felt so natural, so right, now. He seemed to realize that, because he filled her mouth with his tongue, then palmed and kneaded her tender flesh, pushing her harder against his ripening erection with every stroke.

No longer content not to be able to touch him, she wedged her hand between their bodies to cup the full length of him in her palm. He murmured a satisfied sound in response and moved his hips against her hand, silently encouraging her to take her strokes farther still. Eagerly, she unfastened and opened his jeans, too, dipping her hand inside to cover him more intimately. Bare skin on bare skin, the way he was touching her. He felt so big, so powerful, so masterful in her hand, so hot, so hard, so smooth.

For long moments, they only kissed and touched each other, their pulse rates and respiration multiplying with every one that passed. When they finally started moving— slowly, deliberately, carefully—Kendall wasn't sure if it was she or Matthias who was responsible. Somehow, though, they kissed and touched and danced their way across the living room, through the door and up the stairs, until they stood in the upstairs hallway, surrounded by bedrooms. Surrounded by choices.

Only then did Matthias pull back, as if he wanted to give her time to make whatever choice she was going to make. His hesitation surprised her. Usually, he was a man who, when he wanted something, did whatever he had to do to get it. No cajoling, no seducing, no petitioning, only full-on frontal attack, damn the torpedoes or anything that got in his way. She wouldn't have been surprised if he had swept her up at the bottom of the stairs the way Rhett had Scarlett, and carried her to his room to ravish her. Especially since she'd made it clear how very much she wanted to be ravished.

Evidently, though, Matthias pursued his personal affairs with more finesse than he did his professional ones. And for some reason, realizing that just made Kendall that much more certain that allowing this next step between them, however suddenly it had come—though, somehow, it didn't feel that sudden at all—was the right thing to do.

When she said nothing to object to what he was so clearly asking her, he did take the initiative, weaving his fingers through hers and guiding her to the master bedroom. Once inside, he slipped an arm around her waist and pushed her hair aside, bending his head to place a soft, chaste kiss on her nape that, ironically, was infinitely more arousing than all the desperate hungry ones put together. He pulled her body back against his, his hard member surging against her backside, something that shot heat through her entire body. When he nuzzled the curve where her neck joined her shoulder, Kendall tilted her head to facilitate his action, then reached behind herself with both hands to thread her fingers through his hair. She purposely put herself in a vulnerable position, knowing Matthias would take advantage, which he did, covering her breasts with both hands.

As he dragged his mouth along the sensitive flesh of her neck and shoulder, he gently kneaded her breasts through the fabric of her T-shirt, bringing a sigh of pleasure from Kendall. Then he dropped his hands to the hem of the shirt and tugged it up, up, up, pulling it over her head and tossing it to the floor. Then his hands were on her bare breasts, his hot palms squeezing and stroking and caressing. As he rolled one nipple under his thumb, his other hand scooted lower, down along the bare skin of her torso, his middle finger dipping into her navel as it passed. Then Matthias pushed his hand into her panties, finding the hot damp center of her and burying his fingers in the swollen folds of flesh.

She gasped at the sensation that shot through her then, her fingers convulsing in his hair. Kneading her breast with one hand, he stroked her damp flesh with the other—long, thorough, leisurely strokes that pushed her to the brink of insanity. Her body stilled as he touched her, her breathing the only sound in the room. Little by little, he hastened his pace, moving his hand backward and forward, left to right, drawing circles and spirals until finally he touched her in that one place, with that one finger, in a way that made her shatter. Kendall was rocked by an orgasm that came out of nowhere, seizing her body and sending a crash of heat shuddering through her.

For a moment, it felt as if time had stopped, as if she would exist forever in some suspended pinnacle of emotion, her body fused to Matthias's, her heart and lungs racing alongside his. Then the moment dissolved, and so did she, and she spun around to just kiss him and kiss him and kiss him.

Somehow, they managed to undress each other without ever losing physical contact, dropping clothes left and right, leaving them where they lay. On their way to the bed, Matthias slowed long enough to light a trio of candles on the mantelpiece, something that bathed the room in the golden glow of light. They paused by the big sleigh bed, the candlelight limning everything in gold. Kendall's heart pounded faster as she took in the sight that was Matthias. Strangely, he seemed even bigger when he was naked, his broad shoulders and strong arms curved with muscle, his flat chest and torso corded with more beneath the dark hair she found so erotic.

He settled both hands on her hips as she curled her fingers over his shoulders, then sat on the edge of the bed and pulled her into his lap, facing him, her legs straddling his. Roping an arm around her waist, he kissed her again, the way he had before, hungry and urgent and deep. She moved her hand to the hard head of his shaft, palming him, then began to stroke him, leisurely, methodically, as she kissed him back. Matthias curled his hands over her fanny, matching his caresses to hers and mimicking both in the movement of his tongue inside her mouth.

He turned their bodies so that they were lying on the bed crossways, Kendall on her back and he by her side, with one heavy leg draped over both of hers and an arm thrown across her breasts. He kissed her jaw, her cheek, her temple, her forehead, then moved down to her throat, her collarbone and her breast. There, he took his time, flattening his tongue over her nipple before drawing it into his mouth, confidently and completely. He covered her other breast with his hand, catching her nipple between the V of his index and middle fingers, squeezing gently and generating more fire inside her. Wanting more, she spread her legs and rubbed herself against his thigh, gasping at the new sensations that shot through her.

Matthias seemed to understand her needs, because after a few more dizzying flicks of his tongue against the lower curve of her breast, he moved downward again, tasting her navel this time as he passed and kissing the skin beneath. Then he was going lower still, pushing open Kendall's legs to duck his head between them, running his tongue over the warm damp folds without a single hesitation. He lapped leisurely with the flat of his tongue, then drew generous circles with the tip. Pushing his hands beneath her fanny he lifted her higher, parting her with his thumbs so that he could penetrate her with his tongue, again and again and again. Then he was penetrating her with his finger, too, deeper now, slower, more thoroughly.

Ripples of pleasure began to purl through Kendall again, starting low in her belly and echoing outward, until her body was trembling with the beginning of a second climax. Seeming to sense how close she was, Matthias moved his body again, this time kneeling before her. He parted her legs and, grasping an ankle in each hand, pulled her toward himself to bury himself inside her—deep, *deep* inside her. Hooking her legs over his shoulders, he lowered his body over hers, braced both elbows on the mattress on each side of her and thrust himself forward even deeper. Again and again, he bucked his hips against hers, going deeper with each new penetration, opening Kendall wider to receive him. She wrapped her fingers tight around his steely biceps as he thrust harder, taking him as deeply as she could, until finally, finally, they both cried out with the explosive responses that rocked them.

For one long moment, they clung to each other, his body shuddering in the last of its release, hers quaking with the remnants of her climax. Then Matthias was relaxing, falling to the bed beside Kendall, one hand draped over her waist, the other arcing over her head.

It was then that Kendall's confidence about what she had allowed to happen between them began to slip. Because she realized then that what she had thought was a crush on her boss was so much more. And although Matthias had certainly mellowed during his time at the lodge, to the point where he no longer seemed consumed by his work, he'd offered no indication that he considered anything else more important. Maybe he wasn't married to his business anymore. Maybe. But could he—would he—ever join himself to something, someone, else?

Kendall woke slowly, not sure at first where she was. The sun wasn't up yet, but there was an indistinct golden glow dancing at the foot of her bed whose origin she couldn't quite figure out, so groggy was she from sleep. She felt blissfully happy for no reason she could name and snuggled more deeply into the covers.

Why was her bed so much more comfortable than usual? she wondered blearily as she pulled the covers higher. So much warmer? So much more welcome? And why did she want nothing more than to stay here like this forever? Usually, the moment she awoke, she awoke completely, then immediately shoved back the covers and rose to face the day. She was even one of those people who immediately made the bed, so finished with it was she until nightfall came again. But today...

She sighed deeply, purring a little as she exhaled. Today, she just wanted to stay in bed until nightfall came again. Because something about the prospect of nightfall coming once more made a shudder of delight wind through her.

She was about to sigh again when her brain finally started to function—albeit none too quickly. It did get enough momentum going for her to finally realize what the light at the foot of the bed could be.

Fire. Her bedroom was on fire.

She jackknifed up to a sitting position, prepared to flee for her life, then was shocked to discover she was naked.

Why was she naked? In moving so hastily, she jostled the person next to her—why was there another person in her bed?—who, with a muffled groan, turned over and, with a muffled thump, landed on the floor. And she realized there was something very familiar about that groan...

That, finally, was when Kendall remembered. She wasn't in her bed. She wasn't in her condo. The fire in the room was the light of candles. It was perfectly safe. Perfectly lovely. Perfectly romantic. And the reason she felt so good was because—

Oh.

So *that* was why there was someone else in the bed.

She felt more than saw Matthias throw an arm up onto the mattress, but she definitely heard another soft groan as he pulled himself up off the floor. Then she heard a sound of exasperation as he crawled back into bed beside her. And then in a voice full of concern, he asked, "What's wrong?"

Oh, there were so many ways she could answer that question. Too many ways. And even so, none of them seemed quite right. Going to bed with Matthias last night had been the wrong thing to do, Kendall told herself. He was her employer again, and she was too smart to get involved with an office romance. But being in bed with Matthias this morning felt so wonderfully right. She would have been an idiot not to make love with the man last night, feeling the way she did about him.

Okay then, her feelings for him were wrong, she told herself. Falling in love with her boss? How stupid could she be? But then, only a brainless ninny would be immune to a man like him. How could she not love him?

And that was when it hit her full force. She was in love with Matthias. Probably had been for years. She just hadn't let herself admit it, because she'd been convinced he would never love her in return. And maybe he didn't love her, she thought. Just because they'd made love…more than once…with utter abandon…and not a little creativity…

Oh, God, she thought. Kendall had no idea what to think just then. So she did the only thing she could do. She lied.

"Nothing," she said, hoping Matthias didn't detect the note of alarm she heard in her voice. "Nothing's wrong. Everything's wonderful. Fabulous. Marvelous. Stupendous. Couldn't be better. In fact, everything is so perfect that I want to leave right now, before anything happens to change it. I'll see myself out. Call me when you get back to San Francisco. Goodbye."

Okay, so she lied *and* panicked. It was a perfectly justifiable response. Thankful for the darkness, she shoved the covers aside and started to rise from the bed.

Until Matthias clapped a strong hand around her wrist and pulled her back down again. Then he levered his body over hers and kissed her. Hard. Long. Deep. And then some of the tension in Kendall's body began to drain away.

Oh, all right, *all* the tension in her body drained away. In fact, by the time Matthias raised his head, she was pretty sure it was going to be hours before she moved again. Unless, you know, he kissed her like that a second time, in which case she would probably start moving *a lot*.

"Going somewhere?" he asked, his voice a velvet purr in the darkness.

Not sure she could get her tongue to work—well, not for talking, anyway—she only murmured, "Mmm-mmm."

"Good," he said. "Because we're not even close to being finished."

Oh, my, Kendall thought.

He chuckled softly. "First we have to have breakfast."

Ooooh, Kendall thought. Breakfast. Right.

"And I'm in the mood for something light, delectable and sweet."

Kendall was in the mood for something dark, delectable and spicy. They were going to need a smorgasbord for this.

No! she immediately told herself. They weren't going to have a smorgasbord. In fact, they couldn't have breakfast at all. They probably never should have had dinner last night. Or the dessert that had come after. Or the dessert after *that*, either.

She found her voice and softly said, "Matthias, we need to talk."

He cupped his hand over her breast and said, "No, we need to *not* talk."

When he started to lean down to kiss her again, she opened her hand lightly over his chest and held firm. Less softly this time, she repeated, "Matthias. We need to talk."

"Kendall—"

"Matthias."

He expelled a quiet sound of resolution, then rolled back over to his side of the bed. Enough light flickered from the candles to enable her to make out his expression. But where she might have expected him to be annoyed or unhappy, or even angry at her having halted his advance, instead, he looked kind of dejected.

Dejected, she marveled. Matthias Barton. He'd never looked dejected about anything. Because he'd never *been* dejected about anything. Then the look was gone, and she told herself she must have just imagined it.

"What do we need to talk about?" he asked. Sounding kind of dejected.

No, annoyed, she told herself. He must be feeling annoyed that instead of romping in the sheets a while longer, she wanted to do some girlie-girl thing like talk about their feelings. But she needed to know how Matthias felt. Especially since she understood how she felt herself.

Inhaling a deep breath, she said very carefully, "What exactly happened here tonight?"

He hesitated a moment before answering, as if he were trying to be careful in choosing his words, too. "Well," he began, "first we had a very enjoyable day in town, and then we came back here."

Actually, Kendall hadn't intended to go back quite that far, but he seemed to need to stall for a little more time, so she let him off the hook. Hey, it wasn't as though she knew exactly what to say, in spite of being the one who said they needed to talk.

"Then we fixed a great meal here, with a very nice cabernet—"

In which they'd probably overindulged, she couldn't help thinking.

"And then we went into the living room and looked out at the lake," he continued. "And then you kissed me—"

"No, you kissed me," she corrected him.

"And then we kissed," he went on as if she hadn't spoken, "and then we came up to the bedroom and had sex."

She was about to say something in response to that, when he continued, "Then we got hungry and went downstairs to have a snack. Only we stopped in the hallway to, um…have an appetizer."

Kendall opened her mouth to speak, but Matthias continued, "And then we had another appetizer on the landing. And then on the stairs. And then on the living room floor."

She started to talk again, but he went on. "And then we had a snack and came back upstairs and had sex in the bed again. And then we slept. And then we woke up. And now we're talking. Can we do something else now? Something *I* want to do? Like have sex?"

By the time he finished, Kendall was only half listening. Because she'd heard what she'd wanted—or, at least *needed*—to hear halfway through. "So then, it was all just sex?" she asked.

When he hesitated again, she studied his face closely, wishing the light were better. Because no matter what he said next, she wouldn't know if it was true or not unless she could look him in the eye. One thing she'd learned working closely with Matthias for five years was how to tell when he was being serious or when he was bluffing. But if she couldn't see his face…

"What do you mean *just* sex?" he asked in a voice that was void of any emotion at all, something that bothered Kendall even more than it would have bothered her had it been filled with *some*thing, even annoyance. At least then she would have known it meant something to him. "Sex isn't a *just* thing. Sex is a *spectacular* thing. And we had some pretty spectacular sex, Kendall. To reduce it to a cliché, wasn't it good for you, too?"

Oh, it had been more than good, she thought. It had been more than spectacular. Because to her, it had been special. Matthias, she feared, felt differently. And Kendall felt…

Well, she felt different, too. That was what falling in love did to a person. It made them feel different. About everything. Remembering he'd asked her a question that needed an answer, and without thinking, she told him, "It was nice."

"Nice?" he echoed incredulously. "Kendall, my great-

aunt Viola is nice. The Beaujolais Nouveaux last year were nice. Raindrops on roses and whiskers on kittens are nice. Sex with Matthias Barton? That's not nice. That's phenomenal."

In spite of the way she was feeling inside, Kendall smiled. Then, unable to help herself, she reached over and cupped his jaw in her palm. "You were wonderful," she told him.

"Phenomenal," he corrected her.

"Phenomenal," she repeated dutifully.

He had been phenomenal, she thought. But she still didn't know if he was in love. So she turned the conversation to a topic she knew he would understand.

"Matthias," she said carefully, "have you come up with a title for the new position I'll be filling at Barton Limited?"

It wasn't as strange a question as it may have seemed. He wasn't accustomed to talking about his feelings. Although she was confident that he did indeed *have* feelings for her, she wasn't sure if they mirrored hers for him. Asking Matthias how he felt in that moment would only make him clam up. Asking him about work, on the other hand, would make him talk. After five years with him, Kendall had learned to read the subtleties of his business-speak. Matthias's reply to the question she'd just asked would tell her infinitely more than the one to "How do you feel?" would tell her.

"That's kind of a strange question to ask right now, isn't it?" he asked. "I mean, aren't you going to ask me how I feel?"

She shook her head. "I want to hear about the new position. Details this time. Not vague promises."

He expelled a soft sound of resignation, but replied, "Actually, I still haven't come up with a title."

She nodded slowly, her heart sinking a little. "Okay. Then what does the new position involve?"

He hesitated a telling moment, then said, "It's really going to challenge you. The responsibilities are awesome. There will be days when you meet yourself coming and going."

Well, that certainly sounded…vague. "Such as?" she asked.

"Well, your day will begin early," he told her. "I'll expect you at the office by seven-thirty."

"Matthias, that was what time I arrived when I worked for you before. It's not a problem." And, she couldn't help thinking a little sadly, it wasn't very awesome, either.

"Right," he said. "Of course. A typical day for you at this new job will consist of a lot of different things," he continued. "Lots of responsibilities. Awesome responsibilities."

Her heart sank more. "So you've said. You just haven't told me what the responsibilities are."

"Sure I did. They're awesome."

She expelled an impatient breath, her sadness turning to exasperation now. She was pretty sure where this was leading. Now she just wanted to get it over with. "Could you be more specific?" she asked halfheartedly.

"Well," he began in the voice he used whenever he needed to stall, "for instance, every morning, you'd be in charge of sustenance acquisition."

Any hope she might have still been harboring fled with that, and something hard and icy settled in her stomach. She eyed Matthias flatly. "Sustenance acquisition," she repeated.

"Sustenance acquisition," he told her in a more confident voice.

"In other words, getting you your coffee."

He uttered an insulted sound at that. As if he was the one who should be insulted, she thought. Right.

"No, not just getting coffee," he denied.

"Okay, a Danish, too," she conceded. "Or maybe a bagel, if you're on a health kick." He opened his mouth to object, but she cut him off with, "What other awesome responsibilities would I have?"

Not that she couldn't already guess. But she wanted to make sure before she declined the position. And then packed her bags and headed back to San Francisco. She didn't care if she had to hitchhike all the way home.

"Well, let's see," he said, feigning deep thought.

Kendall knew he was feigning it, because if he was having the thoughts she was fairly certain he was having, they weren't in any way deep. Unless they were in something for which she would have to wear waders, which, now that she thought about it, was entirely possible.

"You'd also be in charge of technology aggregation," he told her.

"You mean buying software for your laptop."

"That's way oversimplying it," he told her.

"Right," she agreed. "Because I'd have to do all the paperwork on the warranties, too. And that sure can be awesome."

He continued gallantly, "You'd also be responsible for environmental augmentation."

"Keeping your desk tidy and well supplied," she translated.

He frowned, but added, "And client satisfaction."

"Planning cocktail parties."

"You'd be my sanitary health liaison."

"I'd make appointments for you at your barber and the gym."

"And you'd be in charge of equipment enhancement."

"Pencil sharpening," she said brightly. "Yeah, can't get enough of that."

"Kendall, it's not—"

"Yes," she said vehemently. "It is. What you're describing is exactly the job I left behind."

"All right, all right," he relented. "I want you to come back to work for me in the same capacity you were when you left. As my assistant. But I'll pay you four times what you were earning before."

"To do the same job?"

"Yes."

"Why?"

He didn't answer right away, only met her gaze levelly and studied her with a look she had no idea how to decipher. Finally, though, he told her, "Because you're the best assistant I ever had, that's why."

She closed her eyes. "I'm not an assistant, Matthias," she said. "I'm a businesswoman. That's where I want to make my mark in the world. That's what brings me satisfaction. That's what I want to be defined by." She opened her eyes again and held his gaze with hers. "I don't want to be anyone's assistant. Not even yours."

"But I can't get through the day without you, Kendall."

"Of course you can get through the—"

"No." He cut her off with even more vehemence than she'd shown herself. "I can't. You've seen me. Look, I know I'm good at what I do for a living. Hell, I'm phenomenal at that. But I can't do it by myself. If I have to be bothered with all the mundane, everyday tasks that consume so much time, I can't get anything done."

"And you think I *like* doing those things?" she asked. "You think I'm suited to that?"

"No, that's not what I meant at all."

She shook her head, not bothering to hide her exasperation now. "Face it, Matthias, you just think you're more important than me. You think you're smarter than me, and more essential than me, and more valuable than me. But here's a news flash for you. Everyone's important in some way or another. Everyone's got smarts of one kind or another. Everyone's essential in some capacity. And everyone's valuable, too." She inhaled a deep breath and finished, "I'm valuable, Matthias. For more than getting you coffee and tidying your desk and planning your parties. I can make as big a mark on the world as you have. And I will. Just watch me."

Nine

Matthias felt panic well up inside him when he realized Kendall was going to leave. Really leave this time. Not just her job, but him. And this time there would be no convincing her to come back. How could she think her job wasn't important? The work she did was crucial. And how could she think he didn't consider her valuable? She meant more to him than anything.

Anything.

And that was when it hit him. It wasn't that he needed Kendall as his assistant to keep him on track. And it wasn't that he needed her as his assistant to be successful. And it wasn't that he needed her as his assistant to make him happy. He just needed Kendall. Period. In his work, in his life, in his…

In his heart.

"Kendall, wait," he said as she pushed back the covers and scrambled out of bed.

But she ignored him, jerking the top sheet from the mattress and wrapping it around herself with an awkward sort of fury that generated a sick feeling in the pit of his stomach. After everything they'd enjoyed last night, after everything they'd discovered, she wanted to cover herself up now. She wanted to get away from him.

She wanted to leave.

"Kendall, you don't understand," he added as he rose from the bed, too. He grabbed his navy silk bathrobe from the back of the bedroom door as he followed her into the hall.

"Oh, I understand perfectly," she snapped as she went into the guest room where the bags she hadn't even unpacked still lay on the bed.

Good God, Matthias thought. She didn't even have to pack her bags. All she had to do was get dressed, and she'd be out of there. He had mere minutes before she was gone for good.

"No, you don't," he told her. "You can't understand, because I just figured it out myself."

She spun around so quickly, her hair flew over her face. Brushing it fiercely aside with one hand, her other tightened where she clutched the sheet until her knuckles were white. Her entire body quivered with her anger, he noted. Or maybe it was with something else. Maybe it was the same thing that was making his body shudder, too. The realization that he'd just found something wonderful—the most wonderful, stupendous, spectacular thing in the world—and were about to lose it, before he even had a taste.

Finally, coldly, she said, "What, Matthias? What don't I understand?"

He opened his mouth to try and explain, to try and put

into words, as eloquently as he could, all the things he needed to tell her. How much she'd come to mean to him. Not as an employee, but as a woman. How he couldn't live without her. Not because she helped him work better, but because she helped him live better. How he couldn't get through another day without her. Not because she knew how to work his BlackBerry, but because she knew how to fill all the places inside him he'd thought would be empty forever. But all he could think to tell her was—

"I love you."

She went completely still at that. But her fingers on the sheet relaxed, and her expression softened. "What?" she said, her voice a scant whisper.

"I love you," he said again.

She stiffened once more. "Don't you dare say something like that just because you're trying to—"

"I mean it, Kendall," he said. "I may be heartless when it comes to getting my way in business, but I would never put my heart on the line like this unless I was telling the truth."

He took a few experimental steps into the room, taking courage in the fact that she didn't back away from him. But neither did she reach out to him. Nor did she say a word.

"I thought I needed you to come back as my assistant, because I thought that was why you were good for me." She frowned at that, so he hurried on, "You know me, Kendall. I've always been married to my business. It never occurred to me that anything else could make me happy. I'm an idiot," he admitted. "But I'm not so stupid that I can't learn. And I finally realize, it doesn't matter what job you do, whether you program my BlackBerry or mop the floors at Barton Limited or…or come aboard as my new VP in charge of Public Relations."

She narrowed her eyes at him. "What are you talking about? You have a VP in charge of Public Relations. Mitchell Valentine."

"Yeah, well, Mitchell's wife is pregnant with twins, and he wants to be a stay-at-home dad, so he's leaving at the end of August. I was going to hire a headhunter to find someone to fill the position, but I think I already have the perfect candidate working at Barton Limited."

Her expression was cautious. "Who?"

Did she really have to ask? Well, okay, he supposed she did, since she had asked. "You," he told her. "I'd like you to come work for me as my new VP."

She said nothing in response to his offer, something he wasn't sure was good or bad. So, thinking, what the hell, he decided to go for broke. "There's just one problem," he told her.

Now her expression turned wary. "What's that?"

"Barton Limited has a policy that bars spouses from working together."

Her eyes widened at that.

"Fortunately," he added, "it's just a policy, not written in stone anywhere. Besides which, I'm the CEO, so I can do whatever the hell I want. Should, you know, two of the executives want to get…married."

It occurred to Matthias then that Kendall had never actually said she loved him, too. Not that he wasn't pretty sure she at least had *some* feelings for him. He just wasn't sure if they were as strong as his were for her.

"You really want to marry me?" she asked.

He nodded. "Yes. I do."

"You really love me?"

He nodded again. "More than anything."

This time, she nodded, too. But it was a slow nod. A thoughtful nod. The kind that indicated she was thinking, not agreeing. Finally, though, she told him, "Then I think, Matthias, before we go any further with this, we need to talk about the terms."

Good businesswoman that she was, she insisted they be dressed for their discussion. Conceding the point, Matthias decided they should also have access to coffee. So after dressing and having breakfast, he and Kendall took their coffee out to the deck, where a warm summer breeze skidded off the lake, and where the golden sun washed over them.

They took their seats on the big Adirondack love seat, settling comfortably into the patterned cushions. Matthias took solace in the fact that Kendall sat close enough to touch him, tucking her bare foot under her denim-clad leg comfortably. Her white cotton shirt was embroidered with white flowers and edged with lace, feminine enough to be unprofessional, another good sign. He, too, was barefoot, his blue jeans as worn as hers, his polo an old, lovingly faded green one that was his favorite for those few occasions when he kicked back and relaxed. They were talking terms, he thought, but for something much more important than business.

"Where would you like to start?" he asked.

She sipped her coffee and gazed out at the lake. "It occurs to me that if I agree to this merger, it's not the first time you've attempted this kind of thing. And I want to be clear that, although I'm not the first candidate for the position you've offered me, I'm your first—your only—choice."

He looked at her, confused. "I'm not sure I follow."

She sighed, then turned to face him. "Two words. Lauren Conover."

He smiled a little self-deprecatingly. "Ah. I guess that's my signal to tell you about my botched wedding attempt, isn't it?"

Kendall nodded. "I tried to be subtle, but you men just don't have the subtlety gene."

He nodded. "That explains a lot, actually. Like how my engagement happened in the first place."

He looked at Kendall, who had placed her hand on the seat cushion between them, so that her thumb touched her own thigh and her pinky touched his. Her eyes glistened in the morning light, the sun flickered in her hair, first orange then red then gold, and her cheeks had bloomed pink from the warm breeze. Her entire being seemed illuminated from within, as if it were she, not the sun, that brought warmth to the day. And to Matthias, too. Because he'd sat in the sunshine plenty of times, but never had he felt the way he did in that moment. As if everything in his life that had come before it was only preparation for this moment. As if this moment signified the beginning of something new and wonderful that would last forever.

How could he have missed Kendall's beauty all those years? he wondered. How could he have missed Kendall? How could he have not seen what should have been obvious from the first? That she was a rare, exquisite jewel amid the meaningless rubbish of his work. How could he have thought his work was the most important thing in the world, when every day she was with him was a sign of how there was so much more?

"Matthias?" she said softly.

He lifted a hand to thread his fingers through her hair, then hesitated, in case she didn't want him to. But she leaned her head forward, toward his fingers, toward him, and he closed what was left of the distance gratefully, loving the way the soft, warm tresses felt cascading over his fingertips. "Hmm?" he replied absently.

"The engagement?" she prodded gently. "You were going to tell me why it happened."

Right. He had been planning to tell her about his now-defunct engagement. Which was weird, because there was another engagement he wanted to talk about so much more. Of course, that engagement hadn't happened—yet. So maybe it would be best to divest himself completely of the old one. Then he could move ahead to the new.

"It was actually Lauren's father's idea," he began. "He and I were talking about merging our companies over dinner one night, and when the food came, the conversation turned to more personal subject matter, because it's hard to talk business when you're eating." He adopted his best professor voice as he added, importantly, "Because as everyone knows, it's an unwritten rule of business etiquette that you should never talk about important things with your mouth full. So talk about unimportant things with your mouth full instead."

Kendall chuckled at that. "Yeah, personal matters are so much less important than professional ones."

He nodded. "You learned well at my knee, grasshopper. Unfortunately, a lot of what I taught you was wrong."

She smiled at that. "As long as you understand that now."

"Oh, I understand a lot now that I was clueless about before."

She lifted her hand and cupped his cheek affectionately. A very good sign. "We can talk about that, too," she said. "In fact, I look forward to it. But first, you're talking to Conover…"

"Right. He mentioned that his daughter had just returned from Paris having canceled her wedding for the third time. Not the same wedding, mind you," he hastened to add, "but the third wedding with a third fiancé."

"Lauren Conover was engaged three times before she agreed to marry you?"

Matthias nodded. "Which was why she let her father cajole her into the whole thing. She'd gotten to the point where she didn't trust her own judgment. And Conover took advantage of that to convince her an arranged marriage would be best."

"And how did he convince you of that?" Kendall asked. "Somehow, I've never pictured you as the sort to mistrust your own judgment."

"Too true," he said. Except that, like so many other things, he'd been wrong about that, too. His judgment, at least when it came to matters of the heart, stank. Or, at least, it used to. "But Conover is a very persuasive man, and he made some excellent points about why it would be beneficial to merge our families as well as our businesses. And since I'd never planned to marry, marrying Lauren Conover made sense."

"Whoa, whoa, whoa," Kendall said. "I don't follow that logic at all."

"Of course not," he said. "You don't have the convoluted logic gene that men have."

"Ah."

"The convoluted logic goes like this," he told her, smiling. "Try to keep up. I'd never planned to marry, because I never planned to fall in love." Something else he'd been wrong about, he thought. Man. Where had he ever gotten the idea that he was savvy? "So marrying for love made no sense to me. Marrying for business, however…"

Now Kendall nodded. "Right. Got it. It's all coming clear now. Anything done for the sake of one's business makes perfect sense."

"It used to," he said. "Back before I realized what was really important. I guess I just never really thought marriage was such a big deal. And when I did think about it, it seemed like the things that screwed up a marriage always resulted from the emotional investment people made in it. I concluded that by not investing emotionally, my marriage to Lauren would be successful. As long as she and I looked at it pragmatically, everything would be fine."

"And what did Lauren think?"

"At that point, she agreed with me. Like I said, she'd been engaged three times because she thought she'd been in love, and all three times, she ended up abandoned. She hadn't wanted the arrangement to be based on love any more than I had. Until she came to her senses one day and realized how unrealistic she and I both were being about it."

"And until she met up with your brother, Luke."

Matthias waited for the stab of…something…that should have come with the comment. A stab of jealousy maybe, even if he hadn't been in love with Lauren when Luke set out to seduce her. Or a stab of anger that his brother, even though the two of them had barely been speaking at the time, would misrepresent himself as Matthias and deliberately seduce his brother's bride. Or even a stab of resentment that Luke had won some misguided competition between the two men over a woman.

But all Matthias felt was relief. Profound, unmitigated relief that Lauren, at least, had been smart enough to know they'd be making a huge mistake if they married. Then he met Kendall's gaze again, and he felt something else, too.

Something he'd never felt before, but he recognized none-theless. Something his brother had ultimately found with Matthias's ex-fiancée, something that had made him pro-pose to Lauren instead. Something that made Matthias realize there was a lot more to life than work.

"Love," he said aloud. "Lauren didn't just meet up with my brother, Luke. She fell in love with my brother, Luke."

Kendall said nothing in response to that, only gazed at Matthias in silence. She had to know, though, he thought. Not only had he told her, but her hands were placed right over his heart, and the way his heart was racing now, as he looked back at her, feeling what he felt, knowing what he knew, she had to feel it. She had to.

Finally, softly, she asked, "And how do you feel about that? That your brother, Luke, is going to marry a woman you once planned to marry yourself?"

"I'm happy," he told her. "Lauren's a nice woman. I'm glad she finally found someone who allows her to realize that about herself."

"And Luke?" Kendall asked. "Are you happy for him, too?"

Matthias recalled the last time he'd seen his brother, how desperate and terrified Luke had been when he thought he'd lost Lauren. Helping Luke win her back was the first time he and his brother had worked together to gain something since… He smiled. Wow. That had probably been the first time in their lives they'd ever cooperated together by themselves to achieve a common goal. That it had been to enable one brother to win the heart of the woman who'd been engaged to the other…

Well. That was actually pretty cool, now that Matthias thought about it.

Things between him and Luke were better than they'd been a few months ago, but they still weren't quite settled. Matthias wasn't sure if he and his brother could ever go back to the glory days of college, the one period in their lives when they'd been as close as, well, brothers. But he was willing to put forth the effort if Luke was. In addition to reuniting what was left of the Barton family, burying the hatchet with Luke would be a nice way to honor Hunter's memory. Hunter had been the one who reconciled the two of them at Harvard, by convincing them that brothers were supposed to be at each other's sides, not at each other's throats. Hunter had, in his way, made all of the Seven Samurai feel like brothers. Shame on all of them for not maintaining that brotherhood after his death.

And shame on Matthias and Luke in particular for allowing the gap Hunter had helped close to open again.

"I'm happy for Luke, too," Matthias said.

"Really?" Kendall asked.

He nodded. "Really. He's a good guy, even if he's acted like a lunkhead over the last several years. I guess, in a way, he had his reasons."

Of course, his reasons had been totally misguided, since he'd thought Matthias had cheated him—both years ago and as recently as a few months ago. They'd cleared the air about that two months ago, here at this very lodge. Now it was time to clear the air about everything else, too.

"Luke and Lauren both deserve to be happy," Matthias said. He smiled at Kendall. "Just like you and I deserve to be happy."

"You should call him," Kendall said.

Matthias nodded. "I will. I have a few things to talk to him about, not the least of which is to build a bridge that we should have built years ago." He met her gaze levelly now, wanting to gauge her reaction when he said the rest. "I also want to ask him about being best man at the wedding. My wedding, I mean, not his." He held his breath as he added, "Provided there's going to be a my wedding in addition to his."

She studied him in silence for a long time, her eyes never leaving his. He had no idea what she could be looking for but she must have finally found it, because she smiled. Not a big smile, but it was enough to tell Matthias that everything was going to be okay.

He hoped.

Finally, she said, "What do you mean *your* wedding? I assume there will be someone else at the altar, too, right?"

"God, I hope so," he told her. "It wouldn't be much of a wedding without her."

"It wouldn't be much of a marriage, either," she pointed out. "Since, I assume you're taking into consideration that after the wedding ends, there will be a marriage hanging around your neck."

He tilted his head to the side, feigning consideration. "Mmm, I don't know. I thought I might wear my marriage on my sleeve. Next to my heart."

Now she rolled her eyes. "No one could ever accuse you of wearing your heart on your sleeve, Matthias."

"Maybe not before," he told her. "But I do now."

She bent forward and craned her head to look first at his left arm, then at his right. "I don't see it anywhere."

Catching her under her arms, he lifted her from the love seat and into his lap, then looped both arms around her waist. Oh, yeah, he thought. Everything was going to be just fine.

"Sorry, my mistake," he said as he pulled her close. "My heart isn't *on* my arms. It's *in* them."

She smiled at that, cupping her palm softly over his cheek. "What a coincidence," she said. "My heart is surrounding me."

"So is my love," he told her.

She smiled. "I love you, too."

Very, very fine, he thought, relief—and something even more wonderful—coursing through him.

"Enough to marry me?" he asked.

"As long as it's not convenient," she replied.

He brushed his lips over hers, once, twice, three times, four, enough to get both their hearts pounding, but not enough to scramble their brains—at least not yet. Then he pressed his forehead to hers and pulled her closer still.

"I think I can safely say there will be no convenience in our marriage," he told her. "Love, honor and cherishing, but no convenience."

"Good," she said. "Because convenience just gets too messy sometimes."

He sighed. "I must be absorbing the subtlety gene through osmosis," he said, "because I'm pretty sure you just told me you won't be running Public Relations conveniently, either."

"Oh, don't you worry your handsome little head about that," she told him. "I know what I'm doing. Trust me."

He wasn't much surprised to discover that he did. He trusted Kendall implicitly. And not just with the business, either. Which meant he was so far gone on her, he was never coming back. All the more reason, he thought, to stay together forever.

"I love you, Kendall Scarborough."

"I love you, Matthias Barton."

"Then you'll marry me?"

She nodded. "As long as you promise me you'll never let anyone program your BlackBerry but me."

He chuckled and kissed her quickly on the lips. "It's a deal."

The first deal he'd ever made that would enrich his personal life instead of his professional one. A very sweet deal indeed. Starting today, Matthias Barton was no longer a man who was married to his business. Starting today, he was a man who would be marrying his love. His life. The love of his life.

Life was good, he thought as he dipped his head to Kendall's again. And from here on out, it was only going to get better.

Epilogue

"So tell me more about this picture," Kendall said.

She and Matthias stood on the stairway landing their last day at the lodge, having made their final run through the house to make sure they hadn't left anything behind. Well, other than some wonderful memories. Which, she supposed, they would actually be taking with them after all. They were dressed for the drive back to San Francisco in blue jeans and T-shirts, hers pale yellow and his navy blue, a stark contrast to the suits they'd be donning the following Monday, when they went back to work.

It would be strange, she thought, having an office on a different floor from Matthias. But at least they would still be in the same building. And the Public Relations office was only one floor down from his. They could meet for lunch regularly. And, it went without saying, play footsie under the table whenever there were meetings.

"Tell me about each of the Seven Samurai," she said now. "I know about Hunter," she added. "And obviously, I recognize you and Luke. But who are the others? Which one is Ryan?"

He looked at her askance. "How do you know Ryan's name?"

"I saw the note in the office," she confessed.

He nodded. "It was waiting for me on the desk when I arrived. Ryan obviously knew that would be the first place I went once I got settled. I tacked it up with the photographs because I figured I'd need a laugh. All that stuff about finding The One."

"You think finding 'The One' is a joke?"

He smiled down at her. "Well. I did then. She was, after all, being so uncooperative."

Kendall gaped at him. "Uncooperative? Me?"

"Hey, what else do you call a woman who leaves you high and dry when you've come to depend on her?"

"You fired me!"

"You quit!"

"But I wouldn't have left you high and dry," she told him. "If you hadn't fired me, I would have wrapped up everything I needed to before going. I tried to give you two weeks' notice, but noooooo."

"And what else do you call a woman," he continued, ignoring her, his smile growing broader, "who refuses to come back to work for you, even when you offer her her job back not once, not twice, but three times, even for quadruple her previous salary?"

"It was the job I quit," she pointed out. "Why would I come back?"

"And what would you call a woman," he went on, still

smiling, still ignoring her objections, "who makes you feel things you never thought yourself capable of feeling, who makes you think things you never thought you'd think, who makes you question everything you thought you knew about yourself, everything you thought was universally true."

She brushed her lips lightly over his. "You guys were in college when you made those universal truths," she reminded him. "You didn't know jack about women then."

"We don't know jack about women now," he told her with a laugh.

She shook her head. "You know enough. Because you know how to make us happy. Now, then," she added, pointing to the photo again. "Tell who all these guys are."

He sighed, but this time when he looked at the picture, the sadness she'd seen in him before was gone, replaced by an unmistakable wistfulness that was captured in his voice. "This is Ryan," he said, pointing to the young man on the far right. "He was here last month and met a woman named Kelly Hartley, who I understand decorated the place."

"She's good," Kendall said.

"Ryan seems to think so, too. They're engaged."

Kendall grinned at that.

"This guy—" he went on to the next young man in the group "—is Nathan Barrister. He was the first one to stay here at the lodge. Then he stayed longer out of the lodge, because he ended up marrying the mayor of Hunter's Landing."

"That was fast," Kendall said.

"Nathan's always been the kind of guy to know what he wants, and he does whatever he has to to get it. Her," he quickly corrected himself. "You know what I mean."

"Boy, do I," she said with a laugh.

"And this," Matthias continued, smiling at the comment and moving to the guy next to Nathan, "is Devlin Campbell. He was always the dutiful one. Still is, evidently. He just got married to a woman who's having his baby. Not that he married her out of duty," he hastened to add. "When Ryan called this place a 'love shack' it was for good reason. Dev met Nicole because she was working in a casino near here."

"Hmm," Kendall mused, "and didn't Luke meet Lauren because she came to the lodge looking for you?"

Matthias nodded. "He did indeed."

"So then this *is* a love shack."

"Only in the literal sense," he said.

"So who's this last guy?" Kendall asked.

"That's Jack Howington. Excuse me. I mean Jack Howington the third. Gotta get those three *I*s in there. He was Special Forces after college, but these days, he owns a consulting firm where he takes what he learned in the service and helps people keep their businesses safe in dangerous parts of the world. Interesting guy."

"Sounds like it."

"He'll be staying here after I leave."

Kendall studied the man in the picture carefully. He was, like the rest of them, very handsome. But where the others all seemed to be generous with their smiles, Jack's was a bit more reserved. Maybe mysterious, she decided. Hard to tell.

"I wonder what his experiences in the love shack will be," she said.

Matthias shook his head. "I don't know. But that reminds me. I need to leave him a note, too."

He turned and made his way up to the office loft, Kendall following in his wake. He withdrew a pad of paper from the desk drawer and plucked a pen from a container full of them, then folded himself into the chair. He tapped his mouth lightly with the pen as he thought about what to write, then smiled. Kendall moved to stand behind him, watching him as he wrote, his strong hand moving slowly, as if he were giving great thought to what he was writing. As he moved down the page, she read what he'd written so far.

Jack—

When I read Ryan's note that called this place a "love shack," my first thought was, "What a load of B.S." But now I think he may be on to something. He was also right about how wrong we were when we compiled our universal truths about women. Remember those? Yeah? Well, now you can forget 'em. We had no idea.

Kendall smiled at that, then continued to read.

As for me, here's what I learned during my month at the lodge: The most important work you'll ever do has nothing to do with the job. And it's work you can't do by yourself. But when you find a partner you can trust, and the two of you do that work together, it pays better than any career you could imagine. And perks? You have no idea…

Have a good month, pal.

She noticed that he hesitated before signing it, then finally dashed off, "Matt."

"Matt," she said aloud. "When I first saw that on the note Ryan wrote to you, I couldn't imagine anyone calling you that. But now I think it kind of fits."

"No one but family and close friends has ever called me that," he told her. Then, after another small hesitation, he added, "But if you'd like…"

She didn't have to hesitate at all. "I do like," she told him. "Matt."

She pushed herself up on tiptoe to kiss him, then, as one, they turned to make their way down the stairs. The car was packed, the lodge was empty. They'd left the key on the kitchen table, as the caretaker had asked them to. Kendall told herself not to feel too sad as they closed the front door behind them and checked to make sure it was locked. She would be coming back in a couple of months to see the place again. To meet Matthias's—no, Matt's—friends. To see fulfilled the dream the Seven Samurai had made in college. She was a part of that dream now, she realized as they made their way down the steps. Part of Matt's dream. Part of his life, just as he was part of hers.

No, not part of it, she realized. And not two lives. They were one now. In work. In life. In love.

And that, she thought, was exactly where they needed to be.

* * * * *

Don't miss the exciting conclusion of the
MILLIONAIRE OF THE MONTH *series,*
Susan Mallery's IN BED WITH THE DEVIL,
available August 2007 from Silhouette Desire.

Every Life Has More
Than One Chapter™

Award-winning author Stevi Mittman delivers
another hysterical mystery, featuring Teddi Bayer,
an irrepressible heroine, and her to-die-for hero, Detective Drew Scoones. After all, life on Long Island
can be murder!

*Turn the page for a sneak peek at the warm
and funny fourth book,
WHOSE NUMBER IS UP, ANYWAY?,
in the Teddi Bayer series,
by STEVI MITTMAN.
On sale August 7*

CHAPTER 1

"Before redecorating a room, I always advise my clients to empty it of everything but one chair. Then I suggest they move that chair from place to place, sitting in it, until the placement feels right. Trust your instincts when deciding on furniture placement. Your room should 'feel right.'"

—TipsFromTeddi.com

Gut feelings. You know, that gnawing in the pit of your stomach that warns you that you are about to do the absolute stupidest thing you could do? Something that will ruin life as you know it?

I've got one now, standing at the butcher counter in King Kullen, the grocery store in the same strip mall as L.I. Lanes, the bowling alley-cum-billiard parlor I'm in the process of redecorating for its "Grand Opening."

I realize being in the wrong supermarket probably doesn't sound exactly dire to you, but you aren't the one buying your father a brisket at a store your mother will somehow know isn't Waldbaum's.

And then, June Bayer isn't your mother.

The woman behind the counter has agreed to go into the freezer to find a brisket for me, since there aren't any in the case. There are packages of pork tenderloin, piles of spare ribs and rolls of sausage, but no briskets.

Warning Number Two, right? I should be so out of here.

But no, I'm still in the same spot when she comes back out, bricketless, her face ashen. She opens her mouth as if she is going to scream, but only a gurgle comes out.

And then she pinballs out from behind the counter, knocking bottles of Peter Luger Steak Sauce to the floor on her way, now hitting the tower of cans at the end of the prepared foods aisle and sending them sprawling, now making her way down the aisle, careening from side to side as she goes.

Finally, from a distance, I hear her shout, "He's deeeeeeaaaad! Joey's deeeeeaaaad."

My first thought is *You should always trust your gut.*

My second thought is that now, somehow, my mother will know I was in King Kullen. For weeks I will have to hear "What did you expect?" as though whenever you go to King Kullen someone turns up dead. And if the detective investigating the case turns out to be Detective Drew Scoones…well, I'll never hear the end of that from her, either.

She still suspects I murdered the guy who was found dead on my doorstep last Halloween just to get Drew back into my life.

Several people head for the butcher's freezer and I position myself to block them. If there's one thing I've learned from finding people dead—and the guy on my doorstep wasn't the first one—it's that the police get very testy when you mess with their murder scenes.

"You can't go in there until the police get here," I say, stationing myself at the end of the butcher's counter and in front of the Employees Only door, acting as if I'm some sort of authority. "You'll contaminate the evidence if it turns out to be murder."

Shouts and chaos. You'd think I'd know better than to throw the word *murder* around. Cell phones are flipping open and tongues are wagging.

I amend my statement quickly. "Which, of course, it probably isn't. Murder, I mean. People die all the time, and it's not always in hospitals or their own beds, or…" I babble when I'm nervous, and the idea of someone dead on the other side of the freezer door makes me very nervous.

So does the idea of seeing Drew Scoones again. Drew and I have this on-again, off-again sort of thing…that I kind of turned off.

Who knew he'd take it so personally when he tried to get serious and I responded by saying we could talk about *us* tomorrow—and then caught a plane to my parents' condo in Boca the next day? In July. In the middle of a job.

For some crazy reason, he took that to mean that I was avoiding him and the subject of *us*.

That was three months ago. I haven't seen him since.

The manager, who identifies himself and points to his nameplate in case I don't believe him, says he has to go into *his cooler*. "Maybe Joey's not dead," he says. "Maybe he can be saved, and you're letting him die in there. Did you ever think of that?"

In fact, I hadn't. But I had thought that the murderer might try to go back in to make sure his tracks were covered, so I say that I will go in and check.

Which means that the manager and I couple up and go in together while everyone pushes against the doorway to peer in, erasing any chance of finding clean prints on that Employees Only door.

I expect to find carcasses of dead animals hanging from hooks, and maybe Joey hanging from one, too. I think it's going to be very creepy and I steel myself, only to find a rather benign series of shelves with large slabs of meat laid out carefully on them, along with boxes and boxes marked simply Chicken.

Nothing scary here, unless you count the body of a middle-aged man with graying hair sprawled faceup on the floor. His eyes are wide open and unblinking. His shirt is stiff. His pants are stiff. His body is stiff. And his expression, you should forgive the pun—is frozen. Bill-the-manager crosses himself and stands mute while I pronounce the guy dead in a sort of *happy now?* tone.

"We should not be in here," I say, and he nods his head emphatically and helps me push people out of the doorway just in time to hear the police sirens and see the cop cars pull up outside the big store windows.

Bobbie Lyons, my partner in Teddi Bayer Interior Designs (and also my neighbor, my best friend and my private fashion police), and Mark, our carpenter (and my dogsitter, confidant, and ego booster), rush in from next door. They beat the cops by a half step and shout out my name. People point in my direction.

After all the publicity that followed the unfortunate incident during which I shot my ex-husband, Rio Gallo, and then the subsequent murder of my first client—which I solved, I might add—it seems like the whole world, or at least all of Long Island, knows who I am.

Mark asks if I'm all right. (Did I remember to mention that the man is drop-dead-gorgeous-but-a-decade-too-

young-for-me-yet-too-old-for-my-daughter-thank-god?) I
don't get a chance to answer him because the police are
quickly closing in on the store manager and me.

"The woman—" I begin telling the police. Then I have
to pause for the manager to fill in her name, which he
does: *Fran.*

I continue. "Right. Fran. Fran went into the freezer to
get a brisket. A moment later she came out and screamed
that Joey was dead. So I'd say she was the one who discovered the body."

"And you are…?" the cop asks me. It comes out a bit
like who do I *think* I am, rather than who am I really.

"An innocent bystander," Bobbie, hair perfect, makeup
just right, says, carefully placing her body between the
cop and me.

"And she was just leaving," Mark adds. They each take
one of my arms.

Fran comes into the inner circle surrounding the cops.
In case it isn't obvious from the hairnet and bloodstained
white apron with Fran embroidered on it, I explain that she
was the butcher who was going for the brisket. Mark and
Bobbie take that as a signal that I've done my job and they
can now get me out of there. They twist around, with me
in the middle, as if we're a Rockettes line, until we are
facing away from the butcher counter. They've managed
to propel me a few steps toward the exit when disaster—
in the form of a Mazda RX7 pulling up at the loading
curb—strikes.

Mark's grip on my arm tightens like a vise. "Too
late," he says.

Bobbie's expletive is unprintable. "Maybe there's a back
door," she suggests, but Mark is right. It's too late.

I've laid my eyes on Detective Scoones. And while my gut is trying to warn me that my heart shouldn't go there, regions farther south are melting at just the sight of him.

"Walk," Bobbie orders me.

And I try to. Really.

Walk, I tell my feet. *Just put one foot in front of the other.*

I can do this because I know, in my heart of hearts, that if Drew Scoones was still interested in me, he'd have gotten in touch with me after I returned from Boca. And he didn't.

Since he's a detective, Drew doesn't have to wear one of those dark blue Nassau County Police uniforms. Instead, he's got on jeans, a tight-fitting T-shirt and a tweedy sports jacket. If you think that sounds good, you should see him. Chiseled features, cleft chin, brown hair that's naturally a little sandy in the front, a smile that…well, that doesn't matter. He isn't smiling now.

He walks up to me, tucks his sunglasses into his breast pocket and looks me over from head to toe.

"Well, if it isn't Miss Cut and Run," he says. "Aren't you supposed to be somewhere in Florida or something?" He looks at Mark accusingly, as if he was covering for me when he told Drew I was gone.

"Detective Scoones?" one of the uniforms says. "The stiff's in the cooler and the woman who found him is over there." He jerks his head in Fran's direction.

Drew continues to stare at me.

You know how when you were young, your mother always told you to wear clean underwear in case you were in an accident? And how, a little farther on, she told you not to go out in hair rollers because you never knew who you might see—or who might see you? And how now your best friend says she wouldn't be caught dead without makeup and suggests you shouldn't, either?

Okay, today, *finally,* in my overalls and Converse sneakers, I get it.

I brush my hair out of my eyes. "Well, I'm back," I say. As if he hasn't known my exact whereabouts. The man is a detective, for heaven's sake. "Been back awhile."

Bobbie has watched the exchange and apparently decided she's given Drew all the time he deserves. "And we've got work to do, so…" she says, grabbing my arm and giving Drew a little two-fingered wave goodbye.

As I back up a foot or two, the store manager sees his chance and places himself in front of Drew, trying to get his attention. Maybe what makes Drew such a good detective is his ability to focus.

Only what he's focusing on is me.

"Phone broken? Carrier pigeon died?" he asks me, taking in Fran, the manager, the meat counter and that Employees Only door, all without taking his eyes off me.

Mark tries to break the spell. "We've got work to do there, you've got work to do here, Scoones," Mark says to him, gesturing toward next door. "So it's back to the alley for us."

Drew's lip twitches. "You working the alley now?" he says.

"If you'd like to follow me," Bill-the-manager, clearly exasperated, says to Drew—who doesn't respond. It's as if waiting for my answer is all he has to do.

So, fine. "You knew I was back," I say.

The man has known my whereabouts every hour of the day for as long as I've known him. And my mother's not the only one who won't buy that he "just happened" to answer this particular call. In fact, I'm willing to bet my children's lunch money that he's taken every call within ten miles of my home since the day I got back.

And now he's gotten lucky.

"*You* could have called *me*," I say.

"You're the one who said *tomorrow* for our talk and then flew the coop, chickie," he says. "I figured the ball was in your court."

"Detective?" the uniform says. "There's something you ought to see in here."

Drew gives me a look that amounts to *in or out?*

He could be talking about the investigation, or about our relationship.

Bobbie tries to steer me away. Mark's fists are balled. Drew waits me out, knowing I won't be able to resist what might be a murder investigation.

Finally he turns and heads for the cooler.

And, like a puppy dog, I follow.

Bobbie grabs the back of my shirt and pulls me to a halt.

"I'm just going to show him something," I say, yanking away.

"Yeah," Bobbie says, pointedly looking at the buttons on my blouse. The two at breast level have popped. "That's what I'm afraid of."

HARLEQUIN®

Mediterranean NIGHTS™

*Glamour, elegance, mystery and revenge
aboard the high seas...*

Coming in August 2007...

THE TYCOON'S SON

by
award-winning author
Cindy Kirk

Businessman Theo Catomeris's long-estranged
father is determined to reconnect with his son, so
he hires Trish Melrose to persuade Theo to renew
his contract with Liberty Line. Sailing aboard the
luxurious *Alexandra's Dream* is a rare opportunity for
the single mom to mix business and pleasure. But
an undeniable attraction between Trish and Theo is
distracting her from the task at hand....

REQUEST YOUR FREE BOOKS!

2 FREE NOVELS PLUS 2 FREE GIFTS!

Passionate, Powerful, Provocative!

YES! Please send me 2 FREE Silhouette Desire® novels and my 2 FREE gifts. After receiving them, if I don't wish to receive any more books, I can return the shipping statement marked "cancel." If I don't cancel, I will receive 6 brand-new novels every month and be billed just $3.80 per book in the U.S., or $4.47 per book in Canada, plus 25¢ shipping and handling per book and applicable taxes, if any*. That's a savings of almost 15% off the cover price! I understand that accepting the 2 free books and gifts places me under no obligation to buy anything. I can always return a shipment and cancel at any time. Even if I never buy another book from Silhouette, the two free books and gifts are mine to keep forever.   225 SDN EEXJ 326 SDN EEXU

Name _____ (PLEASE PRINT) _____

Address _____ Apt. _____

City _____ State/Prov. _____ Zip/Postal Code _____

Signature (if under 18, a parent or guardian must sign)

Mail to the **Silhouette Reader Service™**:
IN U.S.A.: P.O. Box 1867, Buffalo, NY 14240-1867
IN CANADA: P.O. Box 609, Fort Erie, Ontario L2A 5X3

Not valid to current Silhouette Desire subscribers.

Want to try two free books from another line?
Call 1-800-873-8635 or visit www.morefreebooks.com.

* Terms and prices subject to change without notice. NY residents add applicable sales tax. Canadian residents will be charged applicable provincial taxes and GST. This offer is limited to one order per household. All orders subject to approval. Credit or debit balances in a customer's account(s) may be offset by any other outstanding balance owed by or to the customer. Please allow 4 to 6 weeks for delivery.

Your Privacy: Silhouette is committed to protecting your privacy. Our Privacy Policy is available online at www.eHarlequin.com or upon request from the Reader Service. From time to time we make our lists of customers available to reputable firms who may have a product or service of interest to you. If you would prefer we not share your name and address, please check here. ☐

SDES07